A Lady's Ruinous Plan

by

Lora Darling

Rumor Has It, Book One

A Lady's Ruinous Plan

Cover Art by *Diana Carlile*

The Wild Rose Press, Inc.
PO Box 708
Adams Basin, NY 14410-0708
Visit us at www.thewildrosepress.com

Publishing History
First Tea Rose Edition, 2020
Print ISBN 978-1-5092-3002-0
Digital ISBN 978-1-5092-3003-7

Rumor Has It, Book One
Published in the United States of America

When a lady of great wealth needs to be ruined, only one of the most celebrated rakes of London will do.

Eirene had never considered herself a typical sort of female. She could not recall ever having gaped over the appearance of a man. Though, to her recollection, she had never been in the presence of a man quite so…*impressive.*

Where the devil was the poetic, continental, empty-headed, effeminate peacock she had been expecting? She glanced around the room, half expecting said creature to suddenly appear from behind one of the tall chairs. Of course, that did not occur, and she could not pretend the man before the hearth was any other than Vicomte Benoit.

Taking advantage of her silent stupor, he strode toward her to confirm his identity with a courtly bow. "Vicomte Benoit, at your service, my lady."

As if controlled by an invisible puppet master, her hand lifted so that he might kiss the air above her knuckles. While doing so, he kept his gaze upon her face. And what a gaze it was. Had the papers mentioned his eyes were the color of freshly buffed pewter? Surely, if they had, she would remember. And what of his hair? Why had none of the gossips thought to remark upon the multi-hued golden waves? Perhaps if the gossips knew how to do their job, she would have been better prepared.

"Enchanté." He released her hand and straightened to flash another smile that could have melted butter on a cold winter's day.

Chapter One

Lady Eirene Rowe-Weston prided herself on being a sensible woman. Whenever faced with a dilemma, no matter the scale, she always made a point to weigh several options before deciding upon a course of action. She made lists. A great many lists, outlining the pros and cons, based upon which fork in the road she might choose to follow. This practice had served her well in the past, and she had great faith it would do so again.

The most recent dilemma requiring a list of options had been whether to remain in the country or venture to London. The pros had weighed heavily toward remaining in the country, but in the end, she realized the *necessity* of coming to London. Despite the cons, which had stacked themselves against the move, she was here now and had to press on with Life's Next Great Dilemma. That of her future. And sanity, were she honest.

Sipping her tea, she considered her Great Dilemma, that of a woman in possession of great wealth while having no desire to *become* a possession. In short, she had no wish to marry. Sadly, great wealth came with the label of being a great catch. Looks, manners, intelligence, wit, it all ceased to matter when accompanied by a large, and in her case bursting, coffer.

One need only recall the great marital success

achieved by Lady Rowena Cummins two seasons ago. The young lady had married a Scottish laird in possession of a most important lineage and not a single farthing. The gossips had been quick to opine the lady would be right at home amongst the herds of Highland cattle, given her resemblance to one. Adding, the laird need not look upon his new bride's countenance in order to plant an heir.

Harsh, yes, but it proved Eirene's point. Wealth trumped all other qualifications when it came to eligibility upon the marriage market. Though, last she read, the laird and his lady were quite content with one another, proving the gossips were not always right.

But returning to her Great Dilemma…

"More tea, my lady?" Hamish, her butler, stood at her shoulder with the pot, offering a momentary reprieve from her deliberations. She set down her cup, and he poured without spilling a drop. "A new stack awaits your perusal, my lady. Shall I fetch it?"

"Good lord, no." She'd received numerous invitations daily from the desperately destitute gentlemen of London. "Burn them all."

"If I may, my lady?" He hovered. Hamish never hovered. No, not true. He had hovered once and that incident led to him delivering the news of her grandfather's passing. A death that had led to her Great Dilemma, for it was her grandfather's vast wealth that now found itself in her possession.

Eirene glanced up at her butler. "I believe I will not approve of your next words."

He took that as permission to speak. "Perhaps you will discover a solution to your dilemma if you peruse a few invitations?"

"Really, Hamish, how can a man of your intelligence offer such a ridiculous suggestion? Those invitations are from men who wish to marry me. My Dilemma, as you well know, is to avoid marriage so why on earth would I entertain an invite from any of them?"

He shrugged, a gesture he usually avoided so as not to interrupt the lines of his livery. "Perhaps not all the invitations are for marriage."

Eirene stared, gape-mouthed, as Hamish bowed from the room. Well! What had gotten into the man? Suggesting she entertain an invite from a gentleman who had no wish to be…

She snapped her mouth shut.

Hamish was a genius.

****

"Hasn't this charade gone on long enough, Adrien?"

Adrien Cloutier, Vicomte Benoit to all who occupied his social circle, eyed his dear friend, Cyril Petley, in the mirror reflection. "What charade would that be?"

He looked away to continue fussing with his cravat. The folds seemed intent to rebel against his every effort to twist them into obedience. He'd have to have another discussion with the laundress about her excessive use of starch. There existed such a very fine line between the proper amount of starch and a great deal too much starch. Every laundress should possess the knowledge to know when enough was enough. But clearly Cyril did not hold his servants to the standard one should.

Adrien slid his gaze toward his friend, wondering if

this would be a good time to confess his involvement in the sudden departure of Cyril's valet. The redness of Cyril's cheeks as he drew breath to answer Adrien's question led Adrien to let the matter of the valet lie for a bit longer. After all, what one did not know could not hurt them.

"*What* charade?" Cyril wheezed in exasperation then ripped at his cravat to loosen the sorry excuse for a knot the new valet had fashioned beneath his master's many chins. "As if you do not know of what I speak. This viscount nonsense has to stop."

Abandoning the cravat, Adrien slipped the length of linen free of his collar and exchanged it for a fresh one. He had four laid out in a neat row upon his dressing vanity, but if matters led to him needing more than two, he would cancel his plans for the evening and view it as Fate intervening.

"Are you listening to me at all, Adrien?"

Adrien glanced over his shoulder while threading the cravat around his neck. "If I say no will you cease your jabbering?"

He returned his full attention to his reflection but not before catching Cyril's scowl. It was an expression that did his friend no favors as it made him resemble a giant mastiff, *sans* drool, thank goodness. Sitting across the breakfast table while Cyril tucked into his hearty English fare was mortifying enough. To even contemplate the addition of drool...

Adrien shuddered.

"If you end the charade now perhaps the consequences will not be so great."

Ah, finally. Adrien caressed the pristine waterfall of his cravat then turned his back to the mirror to face his agitated friend. "Whether I expose the ruse now or six months from now, the consequences will be precisely the same. I will be ruined, and the promise I made will have been for naught. You of all people know why I cannot allow that to happen."

"Adrien, be reasonable." Cyril heaved his bulk out of the wing chair Adrien had moved into his dressing room so that his friend might pass judgment in comfort. "No one expects anyone to adhere to a deathbed promise with the level of tenacity you have displayed."

The words hurt, but Adrien schooled his features. After nearly two decades of learning to hide his true feelings, Cyril's pronouncement lacked any real firepower. "The English might turn their backs on promises made to the dying, but the French do not."

Cyril rolled his eyes. "Do not wave your French flag in my face as an excuse for your behavior. You are enjoying the game, and we both know it."

"No game, Cyril. This has become my life." Adrien reached for his coat and held it out to Cyril. "If you would."

He turned his back, giving his friend no option but to play valet. The expertly tailored frock needed some coaxing up Adrien's long arms before it settled beautifully along the breadth of his shoulders. He tugged at the lapel to give it the final shift it needed, then shot his cuffs. It was a divine coat, worthy of a vicomte and sure to make him the envy of every gentleman at the club.

"We English might not martyr ourselves for the dead, but we do take being lied to damned serious, and you've lied to every soul you have met." Despite the harsh words, Cyril completed his valet duties with a brush of his palms along Adrien's shoulders to further smooth the fabric.

"What do you think of this coat, Cyril?" Now was not the time to speak of a life full of lies and deception.

He ran his hands down the charcoal frock, paying extra attention to the plush velvet lapel and cuffs. The velvet had been intended for a dress shop and had been mistakenly delivered to his tailor. Adrien had insisted upon having a coat trimmed in the luscious, ebony fabric despite his tailor's belief the velvet had likely been ordered to trim a mourning frock. The macabre detail only made Adrien want it more. Worn with black breeches and waistcoat, stark white linens, and high-polished boots, the coat was a masterpiece of elegance and simplicity.

"I think it is a bit somber."

Adrien turned to his friend and flashed a wide smile. "Would it please you more if I had chosen a bright scarlet fabric instead of this divine charcoal?"

"Since when do you dress to please me?" Cyril resumed his seat, letting out a long sigh as he did so. "No doubt the ladies will swoon and the gentlemen will fall upon their tailors on the morrow insisting all they own be trimmed in mourning velvet."

"Yet another fashion triumph for Vicomte Benoit."

Cyril shook his head. "Where does this all end, Adrien? Maybe I could understand if you were seeking an heiress to marry, but you've shown no interest in marriage."

Adrien shuddered again. The subject of marriage did not warrant a reply. In truth, he had nothing a wife would desire. Yes, he possessed money and a title, but she would want his devotion. Or worse, his heart. Those items had been left in France nearly two decades ago.

"Adrien—"

"For God's sake, Cyril." Adrien rounded on his friend. He owed Cyril Petley a great deal, but that did not mean he had to tolerate an endless lecture while readying himself to go out for the evening. "This conversation has become boring. Cease. I beg you."

Cyril snapped his jowls closed, an action that led to an unfortunate rippling effect of his many chins. Before either of them could say another word in hopes of dispelling the sudden tension, Cyril's butler entered the room.

"What is it, Sayers?" It was Cyril who addressed the man. After all, servants should answer to their true master.

"A message for the viscount." Sayers waited for Cyril to jerk his chin in Adrien's direction before handing over the envelope. "No reply was requested, my lord." He bowed out while Adrien extracted the note and read the contents.

Adrien glanced at Cyril. "Do you know a Lady Rowe-Weston?"

"Not personally."

Adrien reread the message. The lady wished him to call upon her in twenty-four hours. She had included her address but nothing else useful.

"Is that whom the note is from?" Cyril stood at Adrien's shoulder, breathing on him as he attempted to read the note. "What does it say?"

"She requests my company tomorrow evening."

Cyril reeled back, his rather small eyes managing to widen impressively. "Lady Rowe-Weston is a known recluse. What the devil does she mean by inviting you into her home?"

"I haven't the faintest." Adrien dropped the missive atop his writing desk. "Nor will I spend another moment thinking about it this evening." He had much more important things to focus on this evening, such as fleecing a good many gentlemen over a high-stakes card game.

"You should think about it. Lady Rowe-Weston is worth more than half the House combined. Rumor has it she possesses enough wealth to buy back the damn colonies, not that they deserve to ever rejoin the fold, if you ask me."

"I did not ask. I never ask." Adrien picked up the missive once more. "A wealthy recluse."

"Obscenely wealthy."

"Very well. An *obscenely* wealthy recluse. What could she want with me?"

Cyril shrugged. "Rumor has it, she possesses a countenance only a mother could love. Maybe she wants to pay you for a little slap and tickle so as not to die never having known the joys of the flesh."

It took a moment for Adrien to arrive at a proper reaction for Cyril's ridiculous suggestion. "Yes, well, I fear she will have to look elsewhere. I am not about to whore myself to one of your countrywomen like that infamous fellow back before the turn of the century. I cannot recall his name, but you know the one."

Cyril's vague expression indicated he did not have a clue.

Adrien gestured with impatience. "Never mind. I will be late for the first hand if I dawdle much longer." Once more he tossed Lady Rowe-Weston's invite upon his desk then headed for the door. "Wish me luck,

Cyril."

"Does Sam have a chair at the table tonight?" Sam. As in Samuel Petley, Cyril's cousin and the heir to the family holdings. The two did not particularly care for one another, nor could they have been more different. If Cyril Petley was the family mastiff, Samuel was the prized Thoroughbred.

"I believe he does."

"Then I wish you all the luck in the world. Take the bastard for everything he's worth."

Adrien smiled. "I do enjoy your bloodthirsty side when you let it show, Cyril."

Cyril bowed, not deeply of course. A man of his girth could never hope to execute the proper bow depth. "I aim to please, my *lord*."

"See there, Cyril, that's the spirit. *Adieu, mon ami*."

****

The card game turned out to be a tedious affair with little to no gain. Perhaps Adrien would have enjoyed better luck had those seated at the table bothered to pay attention to the cards. During the fourth hand, he'd had enough of the murmurs between the two gentlemen seated opposite him. Westhaven and Kilby could barely place a bet for all their chattering. It was akin to being locked in a room with magpies.

Tossing down his hand—a *winning* hand—he cleared his throat. "Is there something you wish to share with Venton and myself, gentlemen?"

Venton, as in Earl Bram Venton, rounded out the participants of the game. For reasons unknown to Adrien, Cyril's cousin, Sam, was a no show.

Henry Westhaven, youngest son of a west county baron, spoke first. "Beg pardon, Benoit, but Kilby just revealed something I find a bit difficult to fathom."

"Well, that clears it all up," Venton drawled into his glass of whiskey. The earl had the manners of a barbarian and the countenance of a demon, but Adrien liked him regardless. Though he never quite turned his back on the man.

"Venton's right, Henry. That was a bit vague." Adrien took up his own whiskey and downed the remains. Almost instantly, a fetching piece in a low-cut gown swooped in to refill his glass. She and her six friends were on loan from a high-class brothel, brought in to dispel any tempers that might erupt at the tables. Once the games ended, they served a much different purpose, and the woman hovering next to Adrien seemed intent to make it clear she would agree to whatever he fancied. He sent her away with a wink.

Westhaven laid down his cards and swept his gaze around the table. "You gentlemen have heard talk of Lady Rowe-Weston, yes?"

Adrien sat up a little straighter, then caught Venton doing the same. *The hell?*

Westhaven leaned forward and lowered his voice. "If you haven't, I'll skip all but what's important. The woman is obscenely wealthy and obviously in need of company." He winked. "If you catch my meaning."

Adrien glanced at Kilby. "Am I to understand the two of you received an invite from said lady, requesting the pleasure of your company?"

Kilby tugged at his cravat. "Aye." He shot a glance toward Westhaven, who offered an encouraging nod. "She's asked to see me evening after next, but I was just saying to Henry I'm not likely to accept the invite." He tugged some more at his cravat. "If it's something

10

clandestine she's after, I'd think someone else better suited to the task."

Adrien slid his gaze from Kilby, allowing the man some privacy as he turned bright red and continued to fidget with his neckwear. Settling his attention upon Westhaven, he cocked a brow. "When are you to meet with the lady?"

"Five days hence. Damned odd."

Venton stirred, drawing everyone's attention "I'm to wait upon her in four days."

"And I, tomorrow," Adrien admitted. What the devil was the lady about?

"That leaves the third day unaccounted for," Westhaven remarked to no one in particular. "Unless she is allowing herself a day of rest, if you catch my meaning."

"Assuming her reason for sending the invitations is as lewd as you suspect." For some reason, Adrien did not think the woman was after a bit of slap and tickle as Cyril so eloquently stated. Inviting such high profile gentlemen into her home seemed a bit scandalous for a recluse. Hell, placing an ad in the *Times* would draw less attention.

"I know that look, Benoit. What's eating at you?"

Adrien looked to Venton. "None of this feels right."

Venton shrugged. "Waste your time attempting to reason through it if you wish, but I could not care less. From what I've heard, the lady has no plans to marry, and I'm in desperate need of a wife. So unless she means to fill my pockets with good, shiny coin, I ain't interested in accepting her cryptic invite." He saluted the table with his whiskey glass. "Have at it, gentlemen." He excused himself after that, all but sealing the doomed fate of the game.

"With Kilby and Venton bowing out, I guess that leaves you and me, Westhaven."

"And myself." The new voice came from behind Adrien, and when he turned in his seat, he found Samuel Petley had arrived. Sam offered a nod of acknowledgment, then took the seat Venton had just vacated. "I do assume you are discussing Lady Rowe-Weston?"

"I take it you received an invite as well?" This from Westhaven as he busied himself collecting up the discarded cards to reshuffle the deck.

"Yes." Petley offered nothing beyond the succinct affirmative.

"Three days hence?" Adrien's question earned him Petley's full attention, and he was once again struck by the lack of familial resemblance between Cyril and Sam. Yes, they were cousins, not brothers, but still. There should have been something to link them together, but there was nothing. Sam rivaled Venton when it came to darkness, with his near-black hair and jet eyes, whereas Cyril possessed nut-brown hair and eyes that tended to read lighter in direct sunlight. Then there was the contrast in their physical proportions. Sam was indeed the thoroughbred Adrien had likened him to with his long limbs and solid build. Cyril could only be described as stout.

But the differences went deeper than the physical. Sam wore an air of greed, as if it were a well-tailored frock. Cyril would have given the shirt off his back to any beggar in the street. But all that aside, quite simply, Adrien did not like Sam. Never had, and he could not imagine he ever would.

"Yes, three days hence I am to call upon the lady." Sam allowed his dark, unsettling gaze to fall upon each occupant of the table in turn before returning his focus to Adrien. "I suggest the rest of you follow Venton's example and bow out gracefully."

Kilby shifted loudly upon his chair, despite already having voiced his intent to ignore the lady's invite. As for Westhaven, he merely shrugged and continued shuffling the cards.

Petley continued to stare at Adrien. "Do I have your word, Benoit?"

Adrien picked up his whiskey. "No." Truth be told, Petley's keen determination to be the only player in Lady Rowe-Weston's mysterious game had just raised the stakes.

****

The next morning, Adrien was in the process of filling his coffee cup for a third time when Cyril finally entered the breakfast room. "I was beginning to wonder if you were ever going to join me, *mon ami*."

Cyril stopped dead in his tracks. "Am I hallucinating? Or are you really standing in the breakfast room after a night of cards, drinking, and God knows what else?"

Adrien carried his coffee to the table. "You are not hallucinating. I am, indeed, here in the flesh and likely because the night lacked excess of any kind. More's the pity."

After filling a plate with his usual fare, Cyril joined Adrien at the table. "Did no one properly appreciate your jacket?"

Adrien acknowledged the jab with a smirk. "Kilby

nearly had a fit while petting the velvet."

"Oh, I imagine he did." Cyril chuckled and speared a sausage onto his fork. "No doubt he would prefer you trim your breeches in velvet next time so he might have an excuse to pet your—"

"Leave off, Cyril. Discussing Kilby's affectations is not the reason I've decided to join you while you feast."

Cyril gestured with his fork for Adrien to elaborate, seeing as how his mouth was full.

"What is there to know about your cousin and Lady Rowe-Weston?"

Once he had swallowed and taken a sip of tea, Cyril sat back in his chair. "Why do you assume there is anything to know?"

"Because your cousin would have pissed on the lady, had she been present last evening, in order to mark his territory. I wish to know why he feels so entitled."

"To my knowledge, he has no reason to feel territorial toward the lady."

"And yet he does. Can you explain it?"

Cyril thought for a moment, sipped some more tea, then nodded. "Sam has made repeated attempts to call upon the lady since her arrival in London. All attempts have been denied, and I don't need to tell you how poorly Sam takes rejection, do I?"

"No." Adrien had witnessed Sam's aversion to rejection in person more than once. It was not a pretty sight. "Why does the lady continue to turn him away?"

"Because he is pushing for her hand in marriage, and rumor has it, she has no intention to wed anyone. He is becoming rather temperamental over the issue.

Claims the lady is merely playing hard to get. If you ask me—" Cyril suddenly gaped at Adrien. "You told him about your invite."

"Not in so many terms, but yes, he is aware."

"Hell, I'm surprised he did not demand pistols at dawn."

"He's that determined to win her hand?"

Having ignored his food for too long, Cyril took up his fork and filled it with egg. "I believe he is, yes."

"I am not the only one who received an invite from the lady."

Due to his enthusiastic eating, Cyril merely raised his brows at that bit of information.

"Westhaven, Kilby, Venton, myself and your cousin."

Cyril's fork clattered to the plate. "The hell? Is the woman daft? Why the devil would she invite Sam into her home? A bit like granny letting in the wolf, isn't it? And what do you make of the others? An odd assortment, if I do say so myself."

"Quite odd, though if she is as reclusive as you claim, perhaps she knows nothing more than what is written in the papers. If, as you presume, she is looking for a bit of intimacy, her choices appear logical given our roguish reputations."

"Damned odd, I say." Cyril shook his head and frowned at his half eaten meal. "Why the devil would a recluse arrange for a parade of notable reprobates to be seen going in and out of her home?" He cast his gaze down the length of the table. "That's a fine way to see one's reputation dead and buried."

Adrien could not agree more. "I will endeavor to provide answers to all your questions once I've met with the lady."

"So you mean to accept her invite?"

"*Oui*. My curiosity aside, I look forward to further enraging your cousin."

Cyril did not quite react as Adrien had anticipated. There was no fraternal smile or amused chuckle at the thought of Sam being bested. He, instead, fixed a rather unsettling gaze upon Adrien and frowned. "Do be careful, Adrien. Sam might not take kindly to being bested."

"You speak as though it is a foregone conclusion I will find favor with the lady."

Now Cyril chuckled. "When has a woman ever proven immune to your charms?"

Chapter Two

"Your guest has arrived, my lady."

Eirene looked up from contemplating the lists spread across her writing desk. "I assume you have seen to his comfort?"

"Aye, my lady. He's no doubt partaking in your fine brandy as we speak."

"Good." Stacking the lists in a neat pile, she stood, then smoothed a few barely discernible creases from her skirt. "How do I look, Hamish?"

Unlike most butlers, who might have stuttered and refused to answer such a question from their mistress, Hamish considered Eirene for a moment or two then offered a curt nod. "You aren't likely to arouse his passions, if that is what you truly wish to know, my lady."

"Thank you, Hamish." She'd chosen well then in deciding to wear a simple frock of deep burgundy, *sans* embellishment, save for a rather opaque fichu tucked inside her modest bodice. "And what do you make of my guest? Is he all the gossips claim him to be?"

"As to that, I wouldn't know. He seems a fine sort of gentleman, and he arrived on a prime bit of horseflesh. Chevalier."

Eirene frowned. "He is a *vicomte*, Hamish, not a knight."

"Begging your pardon, my lady. The horse's name

is Chevalier."

"Ah. I see. Thank you for the insight." Not that any of it was the least bit enlightening. Given Hamish's love of all things equine and his obvious approval of Chevalier, it was no wonder he termed Benoit, "a fine sort of gentleman." He likely had not spared the man more than a passing glance but could probably describe the horse in exacting detail.

She sighed. Best just get on with it then and draw her own conclusions, though she had already decided *against* Benoit based upon what she read in the papers so diligently collected by Hamish. According to gossips, the man possessed great prowess at the card tables and even greater prowess in bed. She had begun to compile a list of the debutantes who had allegedly lost their good sense, and then some, to the man but had abandoned the task when the names spilled onto the back of her paper. It seemed a bit severe to think one man could be responsible for the ruination of such a great many females.

Turning to other remarked upon characteristics had led her to paint a rather vivid image in her mind of Benoit. Poetic and continental were two adjectives the gossips favored. Empty-headed and obnoxious, in other words. As for his looks, the gossips called him dashing and fair. To her, such words were simply code for effeminate. And when describing the man's fashion, forward thinking and unconventional were applied. God help her, but the man was clearly a strutting peacock with more opinions than sense. The fact that he had allegedly seduced half of London only pointed to the frivolity and senselessness of her own gender.

"Shall I prepare a tray, my lady?"

Eirene hesitated. "I think not, Hamish. I do not imagine this interview will take long."

In fact, she could probably have Hamish send the man on his way with an apology for having wasted his time. Doing so, however, went against one of her grandfather's fundamental rules of comportment. When one decided upon a path, one had to see it through to its end, no matter how unpleasant the terrain.

With that in mind, she made her way to the study, determined to eliminate the first of her Chosen Candidates. Her decision to interview said candidates within the confines of the oppressive masculinity of her grandfather's study had not been decided on a whim. She had considered, deliberated, listed the reasons for and against, then decided the atmosphere suitable for exposing the true nature of the five gentlemen. If the room intimidated them, she would know their opinion of their own masculinity and deduce them too weak willed to follow through with the task she intended to lay at their feet. On the other hand, if the room put them at ease, she would move their name to the short list and give them a more thorough consideration once all the interviews were complete.

Hesitating outside the door, she allowed herself a moment to imagine Vicomte Benoit overwhelmed by her grandfather's fondness for ebony paneling, weaponry, and large, leather furniture. Would he be cowering in one of the massive wing-backs or hovering near the desk, tossing back glass after glass of fortifying brandy?

She opened the door and entered, sweeping her gaze about the dimly lit interior until she spied her guest. Contradicting her imaginings, Benoit stood before the hearth, back to the door, legs braced apart, shoulders square, and head canted back. He appeared to be admiring the large portrait of her grandfather in his regimentals. As well he should. The artist had managed to render her grandfather as impressive and intimidating in oils as he had been in the flesh.

"That is my grandfather, the late Earl Weston." Her statement lacked the usual social graces, but she had not invited the man into her home to offer him tea and empty conversation.

Benoit turned and flashed a smile in response to the unsolicited information given in lieu of an actual greeting. "I had surmised as much, but thank you for confirming it, my lady.

Eirene had never considered herself a typical sort of female. She could not recall ever having gaped over the appearance of a man. Though, to her recollection, she had never been in the presence of a man quite so…*impressive*.

Where the devil was the poetic, continental, empty-headed, effeminate peacock she had been expecting? She glanced around the room, half expecting said creature to suddenly appear from behind one of the tall chairs. Of course, that did not occur, and she could not pretend the man before the hearth was any other than Vicomte Benoit.

Taking advantage of her silent stupor, he strode toward her to confirm his identity with a courtly bow. "Vicomte Benoit, at your service, my lady."

As if controlled by an invisible puppet master, her hand lifted so that he might kiss the air above her knuckles. While doing so, he kept his gaze upon her face. And what a gaze it was. Had the papers mentioned his eyes were the color of freshly buffed pewter? Surely, if they had, she would remember. And what of his hair? Why had none of the gossips thought to remark upon the multi-hued golden waves? Perhaps if the gossips knew how to do their job, she would have been better prepared.

"Enchanté." He released her hand and straightened to flash another smile that could have melted butter on a cold winter's day.

Why had no one mentioned that smile?

Mentally shaking herself, she cleared her throat and squared her shoulders. She was being ridiculous, and ridiculous she never was. "Thank you for agreeing to see me upon such short notice, my lord. Please"—she gestured toward her desk and the two chairs angled before it—"have a seat and we shall begin."

"Begin what, if I might be so bold as to inquire?"

Eirene had to concentrate on each step toward her desk lest she fall prey to the rich tones of his voice and find herself a casualty of weak knees. Reaching the desk, she made quick work of rounding it and taking a seat. After a few breaths, her equilibrium returned in full and she was able to address Benoit's question.

"I have every intention of satisfying your curiosity, my lord." She indicated the chair once more then the brandy at the edge of the desk. "Please. Do make yourself comfortable."

The process of watching him cross the room and flick his jacket out of the way before taking a seat had her questioning her sanity. Only a madwoman would find fascination in such menial tasks. And surely only a crazed female would experience a sudden onslaught of dry mouth when considering the expert tailoring that had gone into Benoit's wardrobe. His tailor had to be an artist to have so expertly fitted the navy blue jacket to the breadth of the man's shoulders and the length of his arms.

When Benoit leaned forward to help himself to a glass of brandy, the jacket did not so much as strain at a single seam. It did, however, fall completely open to reveal a black waistcoat shot through with coordinating blue thread and linens so white she wondered if he ever wore the same stock and shirt twice.

"My lady?" He allowed the carafe to hover over an empty glass.

"No, thank you." She dare not imbibe when feeling so out of sorts.

He nodded, set down the carafe, replaced the stopper, then took up his glass. After a sip and an appreciative nod, he settled back into the chair and crossed his legs. Like most men of his set, he wore trousers in lieu of breeches. They were black and as complimentary to the line of his thigh as the jacket was to the breadth of his shoulders. They also fitted tight enough to disappear into the top of his riding boots without a single crease.

"Forgive my boldness, my lady, but am I safe in assuming I am not what you were expecting?"

Eirene forced her gaze from the man's thigh. "Truthfully? No. Not at all."

He smiled, though the gesture was tempered this time. More of a smirk, actually. "Better or worse?"

"Pardon?"

The smirk grew into the full, butter-melting smile. "Am I better or worse than what you had imagined, Lady Rowe-Weston?"

"What an extraordinarily inappropriate question." As if she would stroke the man's well established ego by admitting he exceeded all expectations.

"Yes, well, I have been known to *be* extraordinarily inappropriate at times." He saluted her with his glass, then sipped the brandy. "This is excellent, by the way." He smacked his lips before taking another sip. The action drew her eye to the shape of his mouth, the fullness of the lower lip, and the slightly less full upper. It was a mouth worthy of the rest of his features, its proportions the perfect complement to his rather Romanesque nose, square jaw, chiseled cheekbones, and striking eyes.

Instinctively, she curled her upper lip inward in an attempt to hide its fullness. She had always detested the asymmetry of her lips, the way the bottom lip sat tucked beneath the awning of the upper. A reverse pout, for lack of a better description. To be fair, her mouth suited the rest of her features as well, considering her full cheeks and pert nose were marred by a smattering of freckles no amount of self-remedy could diminish. A perfect mouth would have been wasted on such a flawed countenance. Had her mother not claimed as much time after time?

She had implored Eirene to focus on becoming graceful so as to distract men from her facial flaws. Woo them with harp music, and they might not notice the size of her eyes or the distance between them. Impress them with a kind, delicate, feminine mind, and perhaps they would grow to admire her "spots." Dance as though in possession of angel wings, and mayhap none will remark upon her short stature.

Blast! Why must she recall such things to mind at

present as though she were a wide-eyed debutante afeard of being rejected? It was Benoit who should fear rejection.

Sitting straighter, she cleared her throat and arranged the lists she had brought upon the blotter. "I wish to begin by confirming a few details about your past, my lord." She glanced up. "Do you object?"

"Do I have a choice?" His smile softened the rejoinder.

"Good." She returned her gaze to the papers, memorized the facts, then offered Benoit her best studious glare. "You fled France in 1792, correct?"

"Oui."

"Forced to do so after an act of violence that led to the death of your parents and older brother, yes?"

"Oui." He sipped the brandy.

"Upon arriving in England, you took up residence with Sir Andrew Petley and his wife and son, yes?"

"Oui."

"You now share bachelor quarters with Sir Andrew's son, yes?"

"Oui." He finished the brandy in one long swallow, then shifted forward to place the empty glass upon the tray at the edge of the desk.

Eirene went on before Benoit completed the task. "If my calculations are accurate, you are three and thirty years of—"

"No." He settled back into the chair and flashed a smile. "My birth month is August."

"August. I see." Eirene took up her pen and made a notation, worrying her bottom lip as she did so. How could she have gotten such a basic bit of information wrong? By all accounts, Adrien Benoit, second son of

Vicomte Jean Benoit, had been born *April* of 1777. She supposed it was easy enough to mistake August for April, assuming the person making such a mistake was prone to do so. She was not.

Holding the pen poised above the paper, she met Benoit's gaze. "I apologize in advance if my next question seems a tad personal—"

"Color me intrigued," he drawled while crossing his legs again and propping both elbows upon the arms of the chair.

Eirene tried very hard not to stare at the stretch of black fabric along the length of one very masculine thigh. "Are you able to offer an estimate of your financial worth?"

Some gentlemen hadn't a clue until they began receiving overdue bills that they did not possess quite the wealth they had assumed. Given the quality and workmanship of the coat adorning Benoit's rather impressive frame, she would not be surprised if he was one such gentleman.

"Might I ask why that concerns you, my lady?"

"You may not." She had decided it would not do to allow the gentlemen to pose questions of their own during the beginning stages of the interview. Their time would be given at the end. "I understand, given the circumstances of your past, if you do not possess the wealth enjoyed by a number of your peers, my lord. It is common knowledge most *émigrés* left France with nothing but the history of their good name."

"I am not destitute, my lady."

Eirene chose to ignore the tightness of his tone. "No? And yet you gamble like a man running from the devil lest he drag you to debtor's prison."

25

He uncrossed his legs to lean forward. "And how would you know that?"

"Anyone who cares to read the Society pages knows that tidbit, along with a great many others, my lord."

"*Do* enlighten me, my lady."

"The purpose of this interview is not to stroke your ego, my lord." As if she would repeat most of what had been written about him. As if he did not likely read the articles over his morning repast.

"What *is* the purpose of this interview?"

Eirene waved away the question. "I shall reveal all, in good time."

"Now would be a good time." He stood. Not only was it a gross misconduct for him to do so before the interview had ended, it forced her to track up the entire length of his form to meet his gaze. Given his height, it was not a quick journey. "I am not a man with a great deal of patience, Lady Rowe-Weston, so if you have no desire to get to the point, I do believe I will bid you *adieu*." He turned his back and skirted the chair.

Eirene snapped her gaping mouth shut and lurched to her feet. "I have not concluded the interview, my lord."

Already halfway across the room, he shot a fleeting glance over his shoulder. "If you wish for me to remain, tell me why I am here." He looked away. "You have until I reach the door." Considering the length of his strides, that gave her less than five seconds.

He reached the door in two seconds.

"Very well!" Eirene clenched her fists against the sides of her gown. "If you would be so kind as to return to your seat, my lord—"

He turned to face her but remained at the door. "I can hear just fine from here." The insufferable man crossed his arms and leaned against the doorframe.

Eirene swallowed a scream of frustration. Not only did the man lack the common courtesy to be the prancing, empty-headed peacock she had expected, he had the audacity to be bull-headed, arrogant, and distractingly handsome. Leaning against the doorframe, dressed in navy and black with his arms and ankles crossed, his lush mouth smirking, his golden hair catching the light of the lamp mounted above his shoulder, he looked like a pirate, lacking only a cutlass at his hip.

"My lady?"

She ground her teeth. "I have asked you here in order to determine if you are the best candidate to perform a necessary task."

"The other candidates being, Petley, Westhaven, Venton and Kilby."

"How did you—"

"We gentlemen talk amongst ourselves, my lady, and it's not always about cards, horses, and women."

"I see." Why had she not considered the gentlemen would find out about one another? The papers did label them as mates, after all. How could she have failed to recognize the implications of that designation? And how, if at all, did it alter things? Blast! If ever there was a time for a good list, it was now, but she could not set about the task with Benoit glowering at her from across the room. "Will you return to your seat now that I have satisfied your conditions?"

"You have failed to give any satisfaction." He had the audacity to sweep his gaze up and down her person.

"Though I imagine you could."

Heat blossomed in Eirene's face. Heat prompted by anger over his leering and innuendo. Yes. Anger. To blame it on any other emotion was just downright ridiculous. "I have decided you will not suit at all, my lord. I do thank you for your time. Hamish will—"

"Ah." He pushed away from the door and strolled back across the room with a languid stride that recalled to mind her silly comparison of him to a pirate. Only now she imagined the cutlass clutched in his teeth and perhaps his cravat gone missing and his shirt undone.

Really! She had never possessed the slightest inclination to be fanciful. A handful of minutes in Benoit's presence and suddenly her whimsy was second only to a female who filled her mind with tales of romance and happily ever after.

She made a mental note to order Hamish to have the room aired thoroughly. Clearly some invisible to the senses noxious odor had made its way inside. A logical explanation for her illogical thoughts.

"Am I being dismissed because I noticed you are a woman?" He halted before the desk and once more raked her with his dark gaze. "A fetching woman."

"Do not be ridiculous, my lord. I did nothing to disguise my gender so why would you not notice?" Fetching. He had called her fetching. Her grandfather had always labeled her intelligent, quick-witted, and keen. Her mother and father…well, never mind them. Suffice to say, no one had ever called her fetching.

"True, you are not wearing trousers and a waistcoat, but there are other ways to disguise one's womanly charms." His gaze fell to her bosom. "That fichu, for example."

Eirene touched the length of fabric tucked into the top of her bodice. "What is the matter with my fichu?" Good lord, had she spilled tea on—

"I do not care for it."

He did not care for it? Who the devil asked his opinion on matters concerning her wardrobe choices? Who did the man think he was? "If we are to swap unsolicited opinions upon one another's wardrobe choices, allow me to confess a great dislike for your coat."

"My coat?" He looked down at the expertly tailored garment, then at her with wide eyes. "What the blazes is wrong with my coat? Do you have any idea what a piece like this costs?" He ran a hand lovingly down the front. "I fear you have no taste, my lady."

He was right. There was not a single thing wrong with his coat, but she'd been unable to form a more plausible complaint in regards to his person.

Still stroking the velvety lapels, he leveled a rather disconcerting gaze upon her. "If it truly offends you, my lady, do allow me to dispose of it." Before she could say yay or nay, he worked the garment down his arms. It seemed a task best carried out with an extra set of hands, but he managed with only minimal struggles. Rather lovingly, he laid the coat over the back of his vacated chair.

Eirene almost smiled at his exaggerated show of affection for an article of clothing. The man had missed his calling as an actor. The wayward thought wiped the smile from her face. Her grandfather had always insisted that one never formed a thought that did not warrant further investigation. *Was* Benoit's behavior an act? Was it possible he was more or *less* than he wished her to believe? The puzzle forced her to take a more studied approach in her observation of the man. Given the way his fingers caressed the coat, he certainly appeared genuine in his regard for the frock. But then he dropped his hand, rolled his shoulders, and sighed.

For the second time since entering the study, she gaped. Without the coat, Benoit seemed much altered. He became rather unrestrained, for lack of a better adjective. Of course, the garment had been snug as evidenced by the work it had required for him to remove it, but she dismissed that excuse. The man before her had transformed, and heaven help her, it made him *interesting*.

She had half a mind to order him to put the coat back on, if only to allow her a moment to gather her thoughts. Of course, she did no such thing because a lady would not. It had nothing to do with how much she enjoyed the sight of Benoit in his waistcoat and shirtsleeves.

"Your turn," he announced without warning, with a flick of his hand in the general vicinity of her person. "Fair is fair."

Good heavens! Did the man mean for her to remove her gown? "My lord, you cannot possibly be suggesting what I suspect you are sug—"

He reached across the desk and plucked the fichu free. The boldness of his action, the sheer audacity of it, rendered her speechless. While he slid the light fabric from around her neck, he held her gaze. "*Now* we are even."

Eirene glanced down at the exposed, upper swells of her breasts. She had always believed she possessed too much bosom for a woman blessed with sharp wit and keen intelligence. Such bounty would have better served a different sort of female. Though her mother had believed a good bosom could attract a man's attention who might otherwise be inclined to look elsewhere. She need only utilize said bosom to the best of its potential. Despite her mother's sage advice, she had vowed to never use her bosom in such a base fashion.

A coal shifted in the fire, sending a draft of heated air toward the desk and across her exposed flesh. Her nipples tightened. She drew her attention back to Benoit and expected to find him ogling her cleavage. Instead, he looked her directly in the eyes.

"Whoever invented this scrap of modesty"—he lifted his hand to indicate the fichu balled in his fist— "deserves to be drawn and quartered."

Eirene chose to interpret his words as crass though she suspected they were intended as a compliment. "Exposing me in such a fashion is hardly equivalent to you removing your coat."

Now why the blazes had she said that? It sounded like a challenge, and Benoit looked like a man willing to face any challenge. Heaven help her.

He dropped the fichu atop the desk and reached for the knot of his cravat. Still holding her gaze, he undid the knot, then the buttons of his collar. He spread the fabric wide enough to expose a tantalizing glimpse of collarbone. "Better?"

"You misunderstood my—" Eirene forced her gaze to the man's face. His smile nearly blinded her.

"Are we even now or should I expose more?"

"More?"

He winked. "Only if you tell me why I am here."

Was he determined to purposely misunderstand everything she said? "My lord, I—"

"Why have you invited me into your home, my lady? Given your reaction to the removal of my clothing, I assume it is not for reasons of a base nature."

In an effort to allow herself a much needed moment to consider his assumptions, Eirene averted her gaze, letting her focus fall where it would. Odd, she had never considered her own collarbone to be all that interesting, but Benoit's drew her attention like a bee to pollen.

"I will gladly satisfy the hungry curiosity on your face, my lady, if you solve the riddle of why I am here."

It was rather ungentlemanly of him to continue to barter with the promise of removing more clothing. Likewise, it would be highly improper for her to admit she wished to see more.

She found his gaze. "I need to be ruined." Not the most tactful way to present her dilemma, but tact seemed to have misplaced its invite this evening.

"Financially?" Was that hope she heard in his tone?

She shook her head. "No. Socially."

He narrowed his pewter eyes. "I am not quite certain I fully understand."

"I need to be ruined in the eyes of Society." She sat down, suddenly feeling a bit lightheaded. Maybe she should have run through everything out loud before meeting with the first candidate?

"How? Exactly."

Eirene gazed up at Benoit. Was the man truly that daft? "Really, my lord, must I draw a picture? I need to be discovered in a compromising position, one too scandalous to be forgiven."

He regained his seat as well. "You want me to compromise you?"

"Well, I have not decided if you will be the one, but yes, that is the plan."

Chapter Three

Adrien stared at the woman behind the desk. She wished to be compromised. By him. No. *Possibly* by him. And if not him, then by Westhaven, Kilby, Petley, or Venton. Good God. Amongst such company, he actually emerged the shiniest coin, if one could believe it.

"I have shocked you."

"Oui." Why lie? She had, indeed, shocked him. From the moment she walked into the study. Thanks to Cyril's enlightening gossip about the woman, Adrien had braced himself to come face to face with a "countenance only a mother could love." Cyril deserved to be dunked in the Thames for giving life to such a falsehood.

Lady Rowe-Weston possessed a beauty worthy of inspiring sonnets. Had he fancied himself a poet, he might compare her to a warm summer day or a refreshing gust of wind on a sultry night.

Mon Dieu. The woman had turned him into a minstrel. And a bad one. But who would blame him? Lady Rowe-Weston *was* extraordinary, from her plump lips to her generous cleavage, down to the swell of her hips that could not be disguised under the shapeless sheath gown. In a Society overrun with willowy, thin-lipped beauties, Lady Rowe-Weston was a gust of fresh air on a sultry night. *Jesu*, he was repeating himself.

"I will admit I was rather shocked myself when I decided upon this course of action."

Adrien continued to stare as the woman talked. Her tone was a bit too conversational, considering the conversation. It wasn't as if she had just invited him to a garden party, after all.

"Actually, it was Hamish who gave me the idea."

Her *butler* had suggested she hire a man to ruin her? And Adrien thought Cyril's servants needed discipline? He shook his head, and she ceased talking to regard him with a look one might use to gaze upon a confused child. He was far from being a child, but he was damn confused.

"*Pourquoi? Pardonez.* Why?" Given the circumstances, no other question took priority.

"Ah." She nodded in complete understanding. "It is simple, really. I have no wish to marry—"

"Then simply do not marry."

The poor-sweet-child-allow-me-to-explain look returned to her face. "I wish it were that simple, but it is not."

"Why?" Lord, he was beginning to sound like a poorly trained parrot.

"Perhaps you are not aware, my lord, but I am worth a great deal of money."

"Yes. I have been made aware of the fact."

She nodded once. "Such wealth has gained me a certain popularity among unwed gentlemen, and I have no want of such regard." She held up a hand to silence him as he drew breath to ask another question. "Yes, I could spend the rest of my days rejecting marriage proposals, which arrive daily by the dozens, or I could simply remove myself from the most wanted list. I have chosen to do the latter."

"By hiring me to ruin you."

"I have not made my decision yet, my lord. Nor would it be wise to do so before meeting with the other candidates."

"The other candidates are not qualified to be considered."

"Oh?" The woman took up her pen, shifted the papers around, then looked at him with open anticipation. "Do tell."

Adrien eyed the brandy. Would it be rude to help himself? Did he care? No. Moving to the edge of his chair, he reached for glass and decanter and poured a very healthy serving.

"Do help yourself, my lord."

Without acknowledging the sarcasm behind Lady Rowe-Weston's offer, he took a generous swallow of the damn fine brandy then lowered the glass to rest upon his thigh. "You want me to tell you why you should not hire any of the other gentlemen for this ridiculous scheme of yours?"

"The scheme is not ridiculous, and yes, that is exactly what I wish you to do. You may begin with Westhaven."

"First, tell me how you arrived at the chosen gentlemen." His stipulation left her visibly irritated, an expression that furrowed her dark russet brows and crinkled the freckled bridge of her pert nose. She had the coloring of a field fox, right down to her flashing copper eyes.

"I chose based upon certain criteria I deemed most important."

Adrien bit back a smile. "I'm afraid I shall require

a bit more of an explanation."

A heavy sigh ruffled an errant lock of hair near the corner of her mouth. "All the gentlemen I chose are rumored to be loose with their morals, uncaring of their reputations, and in need of funds, to one degree or another."

"Do you make it a habit to believe everything you read in the gossip rags, my lady? Pardon my boldness, but you do not seem the type to read such tripe."

Her shoulders drew back, and her chin went up a notch. "I do not care what *type* I seem to you. I did my research and arrived at five names. Now. Tell me why Westhaven is a poor choice."

"Westhaven is in love. Madly in love. You could offer him your entire fortune, and he would not agree to partake in your scheme."

"I see." She scribbled quickly upon her paper, then finished by drawing two very decisive lines through what he assumed was Westhaven's name. "What of Kilby?"

"If you knew him, you would not need to ask." Kilby would eventually wed and produce an heir but not until the last possible moment. Until then the man would continue to covet the exacting fashion of men like Adrien while pretending *not* to covet men like Adrien. No one spoke of Kilby's preferences, but everyone either knew or suspected. The man lived a dangerous, dual life, and Adrien would not be the one to hand over such damning ammunition.

"I am not acquainted with him, so I must ask you to explain."

"No." Adrien took a sip of brandy. "Who is next?"

Lady Rowe-Weston frowned, drawing his attention

to her plump mouth. He liked the way her upper lip was slightly fuller than the lower. "We shall revisit the matter of Kilby—"

"And my answer will remain the same."

Her frown deepened, but she did not press the matter. "What of Venton?"

Adrien laughed around another sip of brandy. "Honestly? The man would probably ruin you free of charge, *but*," he stressed as her expression lit up with hope, "he is hunting for a bride because of some nonsense involving his inheritance. He cannot afford to dally where marriage is not an option." He gestured with the glass. "Might as well strike him from the list."

She did so, frowning the entire time. "This is becoming rather discouraging. I am left with only you and Petley."

"Your tone suggests that is akin to choosing between death by hanging or by firing squad."

She looked up though her lashes, allowing him to contemplate the freckles that marched across her nose and along the apples of her cheeks. Not to mention the way her thick lashes framed her large, wide-spaced eyes. "You are partially correct. Petley has been quite tenacious in his attempts to secure a meeting with me."

"I was recently informed he wishes to marry you."

"Yes, and claims he is willing to do so sight unseen." She lifted her head to look at him directly. "He must be incredibly destitute."

"Not in the least," Adrien countered. "The man is simply greedy and dishonest." He shifted forward. "Tell me. Why include him on your list if his determination to marry you has been so obvious?"

She sighed. Deeply. The gesture did extraordinary

things to her bosom, and Adrien could not help but notice. "If he had become my final choice, I would have paid whatever necessary to extinguish any hope he harbored in regards to marriage."

Adrien drew his gaze from the flawless skin of Lady Rowe-Weston's cleavage. "Petley would never have settled for a portion of your wealth."

He remained silent on his opinion that Petley would not have settled for just one rendezvous with the woman either. Once given a taste, Petley had a habit of becoming quite ravenous, be it for a fine horse, good spirits, or a luscious woman. Combined with Sam's single-minded drive, the man would prove too much for Lady Rowe-Weston to handle. There was nothing for it but to ensure she chose that which sat before her.

Tossing down her pen, she fell back against her chair in visible defeat. "That leaves me with you, my lord."

"Am I the firing squad or the gallows?" He meant the question in jest, but Lady Rowe-Weston did not so much as crack a smile. Instead, she studied him as closely as Cyril sometimes studied the breakfast buffet. Though he doubted Lady Rowe-Weston contemplated which part of him to consume first. A pity, that.

"You are more the serpent in the garden or perhaps the apple." She cocked her head, prompting the aforementioned errant coil of deep, auburn hair to slide across her lips. She blew it back into place in a manner that suggested she had no idea how seductive she looked. "Yes, you are the apple."

Her gaze left his face to focus lower. He had nearly forgotten his shirt gaped open, but the pointed regard of her copper eyes made him all too aware of his exposed throat.

"My lady?" If she continued to stare at him with such intense interest, he would need another bottle of brandy. Or an ice bath.

Slowly, she met his gaze. "Tell me, Vicomte Benoit, what would the other gentlemen say of you if seated where you sit now?"

Damn good question. He nursed the brandy to stall for time. Truth was, he had no idea what his closest acquaintances would say about him to Lady Rowe-Weston. Cyril would likely tell her he was a fraud with an unhealthy obsession for lavish frockcoats. As for Venton, Westhaven, Kilby, and Petley...

"It was not meant to be a difficult question, my lord. Surely, you know what your friends think of you?" She leaned forward, eagerness widening her eyes.

"I have not a clue, my lady." His answer extinguished the eagerness in her gaze. "They might tell you I have a knack for winning at cards and with the ladies, but beyond that..." He shrugged.

"Interesting." She picked up her pen again to scratch out some notes. About him? About his inability to read the thoughts and opinions of his friends? The not knowing was making her note taking increasingly irritating.

Once she completed her notes, she kept hold of the pen, twirling it idly while looking at him. "Will you do it?"

Adrien finished his drink in one swallow and nearly choked as a result. "Will I agree to compromise your reputation?"

"Yes." She rifled the papers on her desk. "I am

prepared to be generous." She located what she sought and slipped the sheet across the desk. "If that amount does not satisfy, I am open to negotiating."

Adrien stared at the paper without touching it. The figure rendered him speechless. Cyril had not been jesting when saying Lady Rowe-Weston was rumored to be worth more than half the members of parliament combined. Hell, if this exorbitant amount was anything to go by, she might be worth more than the bloody crown. He would be set for life after only one night's work. Not even a night. A woman could be ruined in a matter of minutes. Hell, he need only hesitate upon her front stoop on his way out, and her reputation would be in tatters.

"It would seem you require more. Very well." She grabbed the edge of the paper, but he covered her hand with his. Her wide gaze flew to his face, and her temptingly lush lips parted.

"The amount is so generous as to be almost vulgar."

"Does that mean you accept?" There was a new, breathy quality to her no nonsense tone.

"Do you fully comprehend what you are asking me to do?" He continued to hold her hand trapped against the paper. "I do not think you do."

"Of course I do." She lifted her chin a bit higher. "I am engaging your services in order to render my person undesirable for marriage."

"That is not all you are doing." He closed his fingers around hers and tugged. The gesture forced her farther forward in her chair, causing her bosom to rest against the edge of the desk. "You are paying me for sex." She blanched beneath the russet stain of her freckles. "Do you know what that makes me if I accept?"

"Incredibly wealthy."

"A whore."

She snatched her hand away as if his skin had caught fire. "Do not be ridiculous, my lord. If you accept, you will be doing me a great service. Nothing more, nothing less."

"*Oui*, but the 'great service' I would be doing is sex for payment. I have no idea how you define prostitution—"

"Enough." She shoved her chair back and stood. "If this sudden show of morality means you do not accept the position, simply say so. I have no desire to waste another moment with a candidate unwilling to do the task."

Adrien stood as well. "I did not say I would not do it, just that I do not believe you have thoroughly thought this through. For instance, why go to such extremes? Surely, you realize my mere presence in your home, if remarked upon, is enough to stain your reputation?"

"I do not wish to be *stained*, my lord. I wish to be irreversibly ruined. Now, if you mean to refuse, do so and take your leave."

"So you might choose from those I have declared unfit for the task?"

"Needs must."

Adrien imagined Petley standing where he stood now, being offered what Lady Rowe-Weston offered. A king's ransom to be caught *in flagrante delicto*. Sam would agree without hesitation, of course, all the while plotting a path straight to the parson.

The woman left him no choice. "Very well."

****

Eirene jumped on Benoit's vague acceptance.

"It is settled then." She had drawn up a contract for The Chosen One to sign, but where the devil was it? She rummaged through the papers on her desk. Normally, she was more organized. Ah, there! "I have prepared a contract. You need only sign—"

"No."

Eirene let the paper hang limp in her fingers as she stared at Benoit. "No? 'Tis simply a contract, my lord. Surely, you did not expect to enter into a business agreement without signing one? Without it, how will I know you intend to uphold your side of the agreement?"

He shook his head and leaned forward to brace both hands atop the desk. Eirene tried very hard not to notice the way his hair swung forward or the way his open shirt gaped all the way to the first button of his waistcoat.

"My eyes are farther north, my lady."

There was no stopping the blush that heated her face as she returned her gaze to Benoit's. "I am quite aware of where your eyes are located, my lord." The vexing man had the audacity to grin at her waspish tone. "Why won't you sign the contract?"

"Contracts can be undone. If I agree to participate in your scheme, my word will have to suffice."

"Your word?" Eirene nearly threw her head back to let out a hearty laugh but refrained. "Surely, you jest, my lord? You cannot possibly believe I will accept the word of a known rake over a binding signature?"

He straightened and crossed his arms. "My word as

43

a *gentleman* should most definitely suffice."

"Forgive me for pointing out what should be obvious, my lord, but were you a gentleman of honor I would not have chosen you as a possible candidate."

"Mon Dieu." His expression darkened, and he uncrossed his arms to once more lean across the desk. "Were you a man, I would call you out for such an insult."

"Do not allow my gender to stop you, my lord, but do know I am an excellent shot." Her grandfather had seen to it that she could shoot as well as any man from any number of distances. The spacing between opponents during a duel would prove no trouble at all.

"I fear you are a most unnatural creature, Lady Rowe-Weston." Shaking his head, he helped himself to more brandy. It had not escaped her notice that the bottle barely held a full glass worth. If Vicomte Benoit lingered much longer she would have to have Hamish fetch a cab to see the man home.

"What you think of me does not matter."

He coughed rather violently around a sip of brandy. "Does not matter? How can you believe my opinion of you does not matter?"

"Because it does not. All that matters is whether you will agree to perform the task I have laid before you while adhering to the conditions attached. Beginning with signing the contract."

"Let us say I decide to sign your contract. What are the other conditions?"

Eirene waved a hand with impatience. "There is no need to go into all of that now. I am prepared to send you all the details when the time comes."

He threw back the rest of his brandy and set the

glass down. "What sort of details?"

Good heavens, the man was stubborn. "If you must know, I have outlined the where, when, and how of my ruination."

"The where, when, and...*Jesu*." He looked as if he might regret the last swallow of brandy. "There is only one *how*, my lady."

"Really, my lord, I would have thought a man of your vast experience would know better than most the great variety of *hows*." She frowned at his ability to rattle her to the point of making no sense. "What I mean to say, I have decided how best to conduct the matter once we are in position to do so."

A decision rendered after researching the most common items of furniture likely to be found within the majority of high society homes. Once she had settled upon a chaise lounge, it was only a matter of determining which rooms most likely to boast said piece of furniture. Then it was a simple matter of deducing which homes had just such a room and when the owners of said homes planned to hold the proper sort of event that might lead to the ruination of one of the guests.

It was all rather easy, though Vicomte Benoit seemed determined to complicate things.

"Did you allow for the possibility that the chosen candidate might have a few stipulations of his own?"

She had not, nor should she have. What could the man possibly require beyond the money she offered to do the deed?

"I can see by your expression, the answer is no." He shook his head as if he suddenly found her incredibly disappointing. "You have not thought this through at all."

"We are back to that, my lord? As I have already stated, I have thought through *every* detail, no matter how small or large. It is now up to you to accept or reject my offer."

"I do not accept."

Eirene stared at Vicomte Benoit across the expanse of the desk. He did not accept. He had taken up her time, consumed her brandy, and vexed her to the depths of her soul just to decline.

She sat down, as if an unseen force had swept her legs out from under her. Her vision blurred as she stared at the contract laid atop her carefully compiled lists. What now? If what he said about the other candidates was accurate, she would have to begin anew and choose different candidates. That would take time, delaying her return to the country and prolonging her exposure to London Society. Why, oh *why*, could Benoit not be as agreeable in character as he was in form?

"There's no reason to pout. I did not say I wouldn't do it. Just that I do not accept your terms."

Eirene looked up. Far up, seeing as how Benoit had not regained his seat. She contemplated the hard edge of his jaw and marveled at how a different perspective could bring different features to the fore. Not that she had failed to notice his jawline prior, but it was much easier to appreciate it when it did not have to compete with other, more distracting features. Like a pair of pewter eyes.

She looked in those eyes. "I do not pout."

"You *are* pouting, and I *will* accept only after you hear my conditions."

Relief made her generous. "Assuming your conditions are reasonable, I will consider them."

"Reasonable or not, if you want me, you will accept them."

"Really, my lord, it is not a matter of *want*." Had he not been paying attention at all? The last thing she *wanted* was a man. No matter how handsome he was with or without his shirt undone. She drew her errant gaze from Benoit's open collar. She really had to stop ogling him.

"We will revisit that untruth in a moment, but first, my conditions. No contract and no money exchanged. Take it or leave it, my lady."

She dropped her head back against the high chair to better gape at the man. "You do not wish to be paid?"

"I will not accept payment for ruining you."

"But if I do not pay you…" Eirene frowned. "Without payment, it is not a job, and if it is not a job, then it is…well…I haven't the foggiest idea what to call it."

"We shall call it what it is, my lady. An illicit rendezvous between two adults."

Heavens. Illicit rendezvous sounded rather intimate. There was to be nothing intimate about the matter. Intimacy led to complications, and she had planned carefully to avoid any complications.

"Do not be ridiculous, my lord. Of course, you will accept payment. To do otherwise suggests a willingness to participate for the sheer pleasure of it, and that will not do at all."

"Am I to understand you have not factored pleasure into your calculations?"

"Of course, I have not." Why would she have?

47

Pleasure had nothing to do with it.

"And what if you accidentally enjoy the moment?"

Only a rake would pose such a question. Men like Benoit devoted their lives to the pursuit of pleasure. Women like her did not. "I assure you, I will not."

"Am I also forbidden to derive pleasure from the experience?"

Had his voice dropped an octave or two? A result of too much brandy? "I cannot control what does or does not bring you pleasure, my lord. I only ask that you make every attempt to comport yourself in a professional manner when the time comes."

"Does this mean you accept my conditions?"

"I would be a fool to pay for a service you wish to offer free of charge, would I not? As for the contract—"

"What if I offered you something more binding than a signature?"

"Such as?" As far as she knew, no such thing existed.

"I will give you the power to ruin me in return."

Chapter Four

Adrien had no idea what had come over him. He blamed Lady Rowe-Weston. The woman smelled like a field of wildflowers. What man wouldn't be discombobulated by such a fragrance? Add to that her fetching looks, and he'd been doomed to make a fool of himself from the start. Top that fact off with copious amounts of brandy, and he was surprised he hadn't made some ill-advised advance upon her person.

Unless one counted the removal of her fichu as an advance. Though she had not seemed particularly offended, especially when he had returned the favor by loosening his cravat and undoing his shirt. He had not missed the way her gaze strayed, time after time, to his throat. The lady might claim she had not planned for pleasure, but he would bet Cyril's finest horse she would be keen to experience some once introduced to the concept.

But to return to the matter at hand. That of his moment of madness. What had he been thinking to suggest he would offer her the means to ruin him in return?

"It is my understanding, my lord, it is near impossible to ruin the reputation of an established rake. Or of any man, for that matter. Your gender is forgiven nearly every indiscretion, so whatever it is you think to offer, I must question if it would truly ruin you."

"What if I told you I am not who you think I am?" And with that, he made it too late to change his mind.

Lady Rowe-Weston blinked. "If that is the case, it would explain the discrepancy of your birth month while affirming my attention to detail."

The woman never said what he thought she would. It made for a damn confusing conversation, not to mention unpredictable. "Most women would take this opportunity to ask *who* am I really."

"Yes, I imagine they might, but you seem keen to drag out the drama of it all, so I will simply be patient and allow you the moment." She folded her hands together atop the desk.

Adrien stifled a growl of frustration. The longer he remained in Lady Rowe-Weston's presence the more he admired her for realizing she should avoid marriage. She would drive a husband mad within a week's time. Assuming the poor bloke lasted a week. Adrien had been in the woman's company for under an hour and had already begun to debate the merits of throwing himself out a window.

"I am breathless with anticipation, my lord." Her cool composure claimed otherwise, but Adrien refused to rise to every sliver of bait thrown his way.

"I am not a lord." There. It was done. His great secret was out. Wouldn't Cyril be proud?

"No offense intended, but I am not entirely surprised by your revelation. You lack the polish of a true aristocrat, polish that no amount of tailoring—" She cast a glance toward his discarded coat. "—will give you. Once you removed that frock, you became an entirely new person, one much more comfortable and, dare I say, common."

Adrien gaped at the woman. Had she really called him common? That was twice now she had offered an insult worthy of a challenge. Never mind the fact he *was* a commoner.

"So it would seem we have reached an agreement, my l—*monsieur*."

"Not so fast, my lady." His words halted her in midmotion as she made to stand. She looked up at him rather awkwardly from her stooped position, then slowly lowered herself back into the chair. "I have given you nothing ruinous."

"You have admitted you are not a lord. I assume your acquaintances do not know."

"Cyril Petley knows."

She nodded. "Well, of course, he does. You live with the man. I imagine he knows more about you than your own mother." Her tone left no room for him to question the logic of her words. "Even devoid of further details, if I decided to expose you in the papers, it would cause quite the sensation."

A chill swept over Adrien. *Mon Dieu.* "It would be your word against mine, my lady."

"True." She tapped her chin with her index finger. "And I imagine your word would hold a great deal more weight than mine."

"A gentleman versus a recluse? Yes. I do believe the chips would fall in my favor."

"Indeed. Then tell me the rest of your secret, so I might possess the necessary ammunition to ruin you should you fail to hold up your end of our agreement."

No one could ever accuse Lady Rowe-Weston of being timid. The woman spoke her mind and made demands as though granted permission to do so by The

Almighty. "We have not reached an agreement," he felt it necessary to point out.

"Really, *monsieur*, must we continue to spar? I have heard your conditions, and I accept your ruinous secret in lieu of your signature, meaning, we have reached an agreement." She stood and thrust out a hand. "Let us shake and make it official."

"You might change your mind once you know who I truly am."

"Are you wanted by the law?"

"Not to my knowledge."

"Then, no, I do not care who you really are." She flicked her gaze down toward her extended hand, leaving no doubt as to her impatience.

Adrien clasped Lady Rowe-Weston's hand, but instead of shaking it, he used it to tug her forward. Off balance, she had to plant her other hand atop the desk to catch herself. Her gasp of surprise, wide eyes, and parted lips thrilled him.

"*Monsieur*, what is the—"

"Hush." He reached for her with his other hand, lightly tracing his thumb along her bottom lip. She snapped her mouth shut with a sharp inhale. "I can think of a better way to seal our deal, my lady. A way more befitting a man and a woman."

"I will not kiss you." She spoke against the light pressure of his thumb, and it seemed the friction affected her as much as it did him. Her cheeks flared with color, and her breaths quickened.

Adrien lowered his gaze to enjoy the rapid rise and fall of Lady Rowe-Weston's bosom. Without the fichu, her pale skin glowed against the dark burgundy of her gown. The contrast brought to mind images of milk-white limbs entangled in dark sheets. What would her reaction be if he told her that her gown matched his bed sheets perfectly? She claimed she had decided upon the location of her ruination, but maybe she would be open to some suggestions.

"Monsieur?" Her voice did not tremble with desire as he might have wished. Instead, she spoke the single-word query in a tone that would have brought a hound to heel.

Adrien returned his gaze to her eyes. "You have hired me to ruin you, my lady, *oui*?" He waited for her to nod. "You claim to have thought this matter all the way through, *oui*?" Another nod. "It seems silly for you to balk at a kiss, considering what will have to transpire for you to be 'irreversibly' ruined."

Ah ha! Just as he suspected. She had *not* thought of everything.

She tried to pull her hand free, but Adrien held firm, forcing her to give up the fight. "Whatever physical contact is necessary to achieve my goal can be dealt with during The Incident. I see no reason to partake in any contact prior to that time."

"Have you considered the very fine line that exists between being ruined and being victimized, my lady? That depending upon what the witnesses see versus what is intended, I might be the only one ruined by our encounter?"

She shook her head. "That is ridiculous. I have no intention of playing the victim."

"Prove it. Allow me to kiss you. Now. With no one watching. If you can convince me you are a willing participant, convincing a stranger should be child's play."

"I will not kiss you."

"Why? Because I am *common*?"

Irritation flared in her eyes. "Do not twist my words in order to use them against me, *monsieur*. I referred to you as common *after* you admitted to not being a lord. It is not my fault if the truth of your situation offends you. Now to answer your original question. I will not kiss you because there is no logic behind doing so at this moment in time, despite your argument to the contrary. The witnesses will believe what is laid before them, and by my reckoning, that will be myself engaged in lewd behavior with you. They will require nothing more damning to arrive at their conclusions." She cast another impatient glance at their joined hands. "Now kindly unhand me."

"What if kissing you changes my mind? What if I find you offensive and believe myself incapable of participating in—"

"Oh for heaven's sake." Shocking the ever living hell out of him, she hooked her free hand around his nape and used the grip as leverage to bring her face closer. He barely had time to take a breath before she pressed her mouth to his with enough force to grind his teeth against the inside of his lips. Just as spontaneously, the kiss ended. "There." She pulled back and swiped the back of her hand across her lips. "I do hope you are satisfied now."

Adrien released Lady Rowe-Weston and straightened on his side of the desk. "What the devil was that supposed to have been?" Napoleon, himself, would have envied the woman's show of aggression but surely not her faulty execution.

"You very well know it was a kiss." She busied

herself with the papers on her desk, stacking them into one pile, then restacking them into two piles before putting them in one pile yet again.

Adrien suppressed a growl and the urge to take hold of the lady's busy hands. "That was not a kiss." Hell, he could probably summon more passion if provoked to kiss Kilby.

She glanced up. "I have no doubt you would know better than I, *monsieur*." Her cheeks were red under the stain of freckles. Was she blushing? Did women such as Lady Rowe-Weston actually possess the ability to blush?

"Any person who has ever been kissed would know the diff—" He stopped. She had never been kissed. The realization tempered his irritation as did the way she returned her attention to her perfectly stacked papers. "You have never been kissed."

"Seeing as how you did not phrase that as a question—"

"How old are you?"

Her gaze jerked up. "I would scold you for asking such an ungentlemanly question of a lady, but—"

"We both know I am not a gentleman," he finished for her. "Yes, yes. *Touché*."

"I am twenty-six."

Twenty-six? How on earth had the woman reached the ripe age of twenty-six, looking the way she did without ever having been kissed? He asked as much.

"How you have managed to convince anyone you are a gentleman is astounding."

"Suffice to say, being in your company has brought out a much different side in me."

"Hmph." She sat down and stared at her paper pile.

"To answer your rude question, I have never been presented with the opportunity."

"Why?" Unless she had been born and had grown to adulthood in an all-female school, she had to have encountered a man at some point in her life. Hell, even if she had not, one of the other females might have kissed her.

There was a scenario best left unexplored.

She looked up, clearly exasperated. "Does it matter? I have never been kissed, so do forgive me if my attempt was less than perfect. Can we move on from this topic now?"

"No." Adrien rounded the desk to stand beside her chair. "Stand up."

"I am perfectly comfortable seated, thank you."

Had he really imagined she would obey? "Please stand up, my lady."

She rolled her eyes and sighed, then stood. "What now, *monsieur*? Are you going to take me in your arms and introduce me to the wonders of a proper kiss?" Her cynical tone might have put off a less determined man, but Adrien had never lacked determination.

He took hold of her shoulders and turned her to face him. She complied with another put upon sigh. He almost laughed at her show of disinterest. Did she not realize how flushed her skin was above her bodice? Could she not feel the rapid pulse visibly fluttering at the base of her throat? Could she not tell she was aroused?

"Go on then. Have done with your demonstration." She tilted her head back, closed her eyes, and pursed her lips.

Adrien smiled and dipped his head toward Lady

Rowe-Weston.

****

Eirene wondered what was taking the man so long. Her neck was beginning to stiffen in protest. She peeked through her lashes in time to watch his blond head descend. Oh, dear! She squeezed her eyes shut and braced herself for contact. Should she have moistened her lips? Should she have opened a window? The room seemed awfully hot of a sudden.

His lips feathered across the line of her jaw. How could he have missed her mouth? Even with his eyes closed, and she assumed they were closed, he should have been able to hone in on her lips. The man was a rake, after all. Rakes were capable of finding their targets in the dark, were they not? No doubt there would be fewer debutantes sent to the countryside each season if all rakes were as inept as *Monsieur* Benoit was proving to be.

His mouth found her ear.

Did the man require a map?

She drew breath to ask, but then his mouth opened against the side of her neck. Heavens!

Eirene instinctively lashed out to hold on to something as her knees trembled. That something ended up being the *monsieur's* coatless shoulders. Part of her hand touched silk, the other part linen. Heat seared her fingers through the thin linen of his shirt. As fascinating as the sensation was, it could not compete with the feel of his open mouth against her neck. His hot breath caressed her skin, making her shiver as if caught in the throes of a horrible fever.

She was not entirely certain she liked kissing.

Benoit's mouth found its way to her ear once more.

"You taste as good as you smell, and you smell like a slice of heaven."

Well. That was a rather lovely compliment. It almost made up for his lack of aim.

He cupped the back of her neck, then slipped his fingers under the weight of her twisted, pinned locks. With the slightest pressure, he coaxed her to lower her chin just a bit. Their eyes met. "You are trembling."

"A gentleman would never remark upon such a thing."

"Have you forgotten, my delicious Lady Rowe-Weston, I am not a gentleman." He found her mouth then, with exacting aim. His lips angled over hers with just the right amount of pressure, no doubt a technique perfected upon the lips of many women before her.

No. She would not think of such things. They did not matter to her. His past did not matter to her. This was business.

She held still and allowed his mouth to shift slightly. The pressure of the kiss increased as did the tightness of his fingers beneath her hair. It seemed logical to respond by holding his shoulders tighter. The linen bunched under her fingers. Her grip would leave wrinkles as if he had been pawed at by a wanton woman.

She would have laughed at the notion had the monsieur not angled his mouth yet again in a way that coerced her lips to part. His tongue slid alongside hers, then retreated almost before she could register the shocking sensation. She waited for him to do it again, but instead, he drew back and released her altogether. She was a tad slower in releasing him, however.

Still holding onto Benoit's shoulders, Eirene

opened her eyes. "Forgive me for saying so, but that seemed rather incomplete, *monsieur*."

He shook his head and plucked each of her hands from his shoulders. "Perhaps it is best if we leave it unfinished until the moment of your ruination." He lowered her arms to her sides and held her thus while giving her an odd, unreadable look. "To answer the question anyone else in your position would have asked, my true name is Adrien Cloutier. My father was a blacksmith, and my mother a lady's maid to Marquise Benoit. The Benoit's second son, also named Adrien, had been born four months before I, and the marquise insisted my mother install me in the chateau nursery while she worked. As a result, I grew up alongside Adrien Benoit. We became inseparable. He was the brother I never had."

Eirene noted the change in the monsieur's tone as soon as he mentioned the marquise's son. She wanted to tell him to stop. His past was his own. He owed her nothing. Instead, she stood silent with her hands clenched in his and tried to remain unaffected by the pain that flooded his pewter eyes.

"When we were fifteen, his parents were murdered and the chateau burned. My parents and Adrien's older brother were inside. None of them survived."

Eirene's heart stuttered. "I am so very—"

He shook his head, stopping her useless words. Releasing her, he strolled away, toward the fireplace and the judgmental portrait of her grandfather. He stood with his back to her so she could not know if he looked at the painting. "It was not easy, but I managed to arrange for Adrien and myself to leave France on an English ship. Adrien fell ill the first night. To this day, I have no idea what caused his sickness." He lowered his head and reached out to brace a hand on the mantle. Said hand appeared to be trembling.

Eirene stood rooted behind her desk. Part of her wished to offer comfort and part of her was terrified to move. She could not recall ever having experienced such a conflict of emotions.

"The other French passengers believed Adrien when he claimed to be my servant. He made all of them promise to ensure I arrived safely in England. I was the sole survivor of a great legacy, he told them. He made me promise to live my life as befitting the son of a marquis. How could I refuse him?" All of a sudden he turned and looked at her, nearly knocking her over with the intensity of his gaze. "So I lied. I lied to Sir Petley and his lady when they came to collect me from the dockside boarding house. I lied to Cyril when he decided we would be great friends in spite of me being French, and I have lied to every soul I have met since. I assure you, my lady, you now possess more than enough information if you find it necessary to ruin me."

Eirene swallowed the lump in her throat and blinked rapidly. "Do you intend to honor your end of our agreement, *monsieur*?"

"I do."

"Then I should have no cause to use this information against you." They were not the words she should have spoken, but it was too late. To offer words of comfort now would turn them into an empty afterthought.

He bowed. "I shall await further instructions." He left without taking his coat.

Eirene collapsed into her chair and pressed shaking

fingers to her throbbing temples. A whirlwind of emotions raged within her. Had she believed for a moment it might help, she would have started a list in order to sort through the cacophony. Instead, she stared at the open study door, then at the forgotten coat. She could not recall the last time she'd felt so shaken or so out of control. Not a single moment of her interview with Monsieur Benoit had gone the way it should have. Things had begun to spiral even before he kissed her.

She dropped her hands and spread her fingers atop the pile of papers. No. She would not think about that kiss or the way her lips still tingled or how she could still feel the memory of his fingers at the back of her head. No. She would not think of it.

Nor would she think about the look on the monsieur's face when he had turned from the fireplace. There had been so much pain etched into his features. If she allowed herself to think about that moment, she would open herself up to another moment best forgotten. A moment she had vowed never to revisit. The moment she had witnessed the death of all her mother's dreams. The moment her father had walked out on them only to get himself killed in an alley behind a public house. Her mother had never recovered from the loss. Eirene had been fifteen as she stood beside her mother's grave, clasping her grandfather's hand. She had vowed that day never to marry, never to play the victim as her mother had.

Damn the monsieur for bringing it all back.

A tear streaked down her face, and she swiped it away in anger then reached for a clean sheet of paper. Dipping her pen, she hesitated for only a moment before beginning a list meant to weigh the pros and cons of having chosen Vicomte Benoit—*née,* Monsieur Cloutier—to see to the all-important, non-reversible task of ruining her for all other men.

****

Adrien slammed into the home he shared with Cyril, nearly flattening the butler behind the front door in the process. His intent was to go straight to his rooms and lose himself in a good bottle of cognac.

"I take it the interview did not go well?" Cyril stepped out of the front parlor as Adrien stalked past. "Where is your coat? And why is your cravat—"

"Go to hell, Cyril." Adrien gained the stairs, taking them three at a time.

Cyril, despite his lesser stride and fuller girth, dogged his heels all the way to his sitting room. Adrien continued to ignore his friend and headed straight for the liquor tray atop his writing desk. The carafe was full of brandy not cognac.

"For god's sake, Adrien, what the hell happened?"

He rounded on Cyril. "Lady Rowe-Weston offered me a king's ransom to ruin her. After a bit of negotiating, I accepted. End of story." He poured a glass of brandy with no intent to drink it. He would never touch the stuff again.

"Run that by me again."

Adrien did not repeat himself.

Cyril eventually worked it out and managed an opinion. "So I was right about the lady wanting a bit of action before kicking up her toes."

"She is a long way from kicking up her toes, I assure you." Adrien set the brandy down. "Nor does she possess a countenance only a mother could love."

"Oh?" Cyril's entire face transformed into a mask

of avid curiosity. "A looker, then?"

"Not in the traditional sense." She had freckles, and freckles simply were not considered beautiful among Society's reigning judges. Those judges could go to hell, in his opinion. Lady Rowe-Weston's freckles were the most beautiful thing he'd laid eyes on since leaving France.

Damn her.

"I'm confused."

Adrien glanced at his friend. "I do not care."

Cyril frowned. "Let me see if I can work this out on my own then. Lady Rowe-Weston, a nontraditional looker, has offered *you* a great deal of money to ruin her, and instead of toasting your ridiculously good fortune, you seem ready to do murder."

"Very good, Cyril. You always were smarter than you look."

Cyril ignored the insult and continued to push. "Is it safe to assume, given your appearance, you have already seen to the task?"

"An open collar hardly indicates lovemaking."

Cyril threw his hands up in defeat. "Have mercy on me, Adrien. Tell me what the blazes happened between you and the lady."

"I kissed her." What a horribly inadequate way to describe what had actually occurred. He had not merely kissed the lady. He had initiated her. Awakened her. Made her tremble.

And then he had laid his life in her hands.

"Since when does kissing put you in such a foul mood?"

"I also told her exactly who I am. All of it."

Cyril stared, then fumbled around for a nearby

chair to fall into. "Why did you do that?"

"Asks the very man who, little more than twenty-four hours ago, beseeched me to have done with the charade. A bit hypocritical of you, *mon ami*. I thought you would be proud."

"I meant for you to tell your friends the truth, not some dried up spinster in need of a—"

"I would not complete that sentence if I were you, Cyril."

Chapter Five

Dearest Reader,

It seems a certain dashing Vicomte paid a visit to a certain reclusive lady yesterday. Given what we know of this lady's vast wealth and what we know to be true of the Vicomte's talents we must wonder what the meeting entailed. It should be noted, the meeting went on for close to an hour and the Vicomte left the lady's home in a rather shocking state of dishabille...

Adrien walked into the breakfast room intent upon apologizing to Cyril for his appalling behavior the previous evening. His friend was not to blame for the disaster that had occurred within Lady Rowe-Weston's study and had not deserved to be bodily threatened for voicing an opinion. Adrien might not be a *true* gentleman, but any man worth his salt knew when to admit a wrong.

Cyril sat at the head of the table, sipping tea and reading the paper. An empty plate sat at his elbow as did untouched cutlery. The sight gave Adrien pause. Had Cyril been too upset to eat, for God's sake? Perhaps an apology would not be enough. A trip to Adrien's favorite tailor might be in order.

Cyril lowered the paper as Adrien entered. "Good morning." The greeting gave no hint as to Cyril's mood.

Adrien decided to jump right in. "I apologize for

my ghastly behavior last night, Cyril. My meeting with Lady Rowe-Weston put me in the foulest of moods, and I lashed out at you. Say you forgive me."

"Only if you vow not to tear into me again once you've had a gander at the gem printed in this morning's Society pages." Cyril slid the paper across the table. "Maybe it'd be best if you remain at a distance while reading it."

Adrien frowned and picked up the paper to read the ear-marked page. Names had been omitted. Names were *always* omitted, but one had to be daft, dumb, or dead not to know whom the writer referred to. *"Mere de Dieu."*

"Precisely," Cyril agreed, though Adrien knew his friend had never taken the time to learn even a single word of French. When in England, speak bloody English, was Cyril's motto. "Despite your denial when *I* remarked upon it, it seems as though an open collar does indicate lovemaking."

"This writer all but insinuates I whored myself to the lady."

Cyril glanced away to pour a fresh cup of tea. "I am more than willing to take your side on the matter, Adrien, but you've yet to explain *why* your collar was undone."

"Why should it matter? Either you believe me when I say nothing happened—"

"You admitted to kissing the lady."

Adrien ground his teeth. "Nothing happened beyond a kiss."

"Many a young lady's reputation has been ruined by a mere kiss." Cyril raised his brows while sipping his tea.

Adrien wanted to smash the dainty mug over his friend's oiled curls. "I undid my cravat and collar to atone for removing the woman's fichu." He regretted the explanation as soon as the words were out.

Cyril nearly vibrated with fresh curiosity. "You removed the woman's fichu? Was it endangering her in some fashion? Surely, you would not have removed it for any other reason, such as to get a better look at her—"

"The woman was an infuriating viper, Cyril. I removed the bloody length of fabric to rattle her frustrating sense of self composure."

"Did it work?"

"Yes and no." After tossing the paper onto the table, Adrien stalked to the side table and grabbed a plate. For the first time since relocating to England, he chose sausage and eggs in lieu of a fluffy pastry. Returning to the table, he plunked the plate down and took a seat under Cyril's watchful gaze. "What?"

Cyril looked at the plate of food, then at Adrien. "Are you ill?"

Adrien speared a sausage and took a bite. Hmm. Imagine that. It was quite tasty. He chewed and swallowed, then went for some egg, which proved just as delicious. "This is quite good."

Cyril looked at Adrien as though he had just figured out the world was not flat. "Although it thrills me to see you enjoying the taste of fine English fare, too much of it will make those fancy coats of yours too tight."

Adrien grunted around another bite of sausage.

"Speaking of," Cyril went on, "where is the masterpiece you wore to Lady Rowe-Weston's?"

"I told you the woman was vexing, did I not? I was in a high temper when I left and forgot the damned coat."

"Should I inquire as to why you had removed it in the first place?"

"No." Adrien laid down his fork, having finished the sausage and eggs, and reached for a cup of coffee. Maybe in time, he would give tea a chance, but not today. Today called for strong coffee. "Tell me what to do about that slanderous gossip article, Cyril."

"Tell you what to do?" Cyril leaned back in his chair. "There is nothing for you to do. It is gossip. You ignore it like the rake you are and move on. Besides"—he waved a hand in the air—"something else is bound to happen in the next twenty-four hours that will be juicy enough to distract the writer from their current interest in you and Lady Rowe-Weston. Mark my words."

****

Eirene shook as she laid the paper beside her untouched breakfast. She had read the column three times just to make sure she had not mistaken the writer's poorly veiled innuendo. Unfortunately, there could be no mistaking the writer's words. The foul author believed Vicomte Benoit had visited for improper reasons, and now all of London would believe the same. As they sipped their morning tea, coffee, or chocolate, they would raise their brows and speculate as to what, exactly, Benoit had done for the reclusive lady.

Damn the man for storming out with his clothing askew. Were he a gentleman, he would have known better, but one could not expect a commoner to pay proper attention to manners and appearances.

"Oh, shut up, Eirene," she scolded out loud. "Had the man not admitted the truth, you never would have suspected he was anything but what he claimed to be. Besides, it was your stupid, loose tongue that led to his collar being undone. Put the blame where it belongs."

"My lady?" Hamish stood in the doorway, eyes wide.

Drat! "Forget every word you just heard me say, Hamish, or you are fired."

"Of course, my lady." He entered the room with a fresh pot of tea in one hand and a stack of calling cards in the other. "I was unable to determine how your meeting with the vicomte went, so I took it upon myself to assume you might wish to explore more options." He laid the cards beside the paper. "On the other hand, if the meeting proved successful, you will wish to cancel your other appointments."

Eirene stared at the calling cards. The one on top belonged to Viscount Petley. Hamish was correct. She would have to send out cancellation notes to the other four gentlemen she had chosen as possible candidates. "I do believe I will wait a bit before seeing to that task, Hamish." She met her butler's inquisitive gaze. "Vicomte Benoit accepted my offer, but I will allow him twenty-four hours to change his mind."

Hamish straightened from pouring the tea. "You believe the gentlemen might do so?"

Before Eirene could respond, there was a knock at the front door. "Whoever it is, send them away, Hamish."

"Yes, my lady, I know the drill by now, I believe." He bowed out of the room to see to his duties, leaving Eirene to contemplate his last question.

Would Benoit change his mind? The man had been in quite a state when he left. Yes, he had laid his dirty little secret at her feet but would that be enough to bind him? If only he had signed the damn contract. At least then, she would have a signature to show the courts if matters escalated to such a degree. Never mind the signature would have been that of a dead man.

She grabbed her tea and gave the contents an agitated blow before taking a sip. "Vexing man," she mumbled around the rim.

"Speak of the devil and he appears."

Eirene nearly dropped her tea cup as Benoit spoke from the breakfast room doorway. Believing she had, in some fashion, conjured him from thought, she blinked and waited for him to vanish. He did not. He remained quite *solid* and a good deal less formal. Today he wore buff, riding trousers, a deep burgundy waistcoat, white shirt and cravat, and an expertly tailored, hunter green coat. The top hat held in his hands was black as were the gloves he had not removed.

"What did you do to my butler?"

"Good morning to you, too."

Eirene eased her grip on the tea cup, lest it shatter. "Good morning, my *lord*. Where is Hamish?"

Hamish would *never* allow a man to enter her breakfast room unannounced.

"Your butler is outside cooing at my horse."

"You have got to be kidding me?" She left her place at the table and moved to the window. Her breakfast room faced the street, allowing an excellent view of Hamish standing at the curb stroking the white-streaked muzzle of a large, black horse. "Why are there two horses?" A smaller, similarly marked horse stood beside the one receiving her *former* butler's attentions.

"I have come to invite you to go riding. You *do* ride, I assume?"

Eirene turned from the window. "Of course I ride, but why would I ride out with you?" Why was he even here? She clearly remembered telling him she would send him further instructions when the time came. The time had not come, therefore, he had no business being in her home, inviting her to do anything.

He twirled his hat and moved farther into the room. His gaze settled on the damning paper, which lay open beside her place setting. "You saw the article." It was not a question so Eirene did not respond. He looked her way. "Cyril suggested I act as though nothing untoward has been said."

"And that suggestion has led you to my door this morning?" What further proof did she need to confirm her belief that men did not reason the same as women?

"I thought if we were seen riding out together—"

"That people would conclude nothing of note transpired between us? Are you mad or simply daft, *monsieur*?" Eirene left her position at the window to stalk closer to Benoit. He held his ground but had the decency to look uneasy. "If we are seen riding out together, it will be assumed you are courting me, and I assure you, you do not have my permission to court me."

He studied her a moment with his unnervingly lovely pewter eyes before responding. "I had believed the assumption you were being courted instead of *serviced* by me would be preferable, but perhaps the lascivious article helps you to further your plan for ruination. If that is the case, I humbly apologize for intruding upon your morning." He bowed and turned to leave.

Eirene forced her gaping mouth shut. "One moment, *monsieur*." He turned back, expression patient. "To make matters perfectly clear, I have no desire to be viewed as being courted or…serviced by you. The grasping gossip writers may think what they wish, but I refuse to give them further cause to write about us until the moment of my plan. I had hoped you would feel the same, but clearly you do not or you would have never arrived at my door in such a bold manner."

He visibly clenched his jaw. "Permit me to say, my lady, I concluded last night it was fortuitous of you to avoid marriage, and that belief has been strengthened this morning."

"*Excuse* me?"

"You are too prickly for marriage, and now that I have been in your company during the evening hours and morning, I know it to be your common state. No man would wish to marry such a prickly female."

How *dare* he? "You have no right to stand in judgment of me, my *lord*."

"I'm not judging, merely observing."

"Kindly keep your observations to yourself in future." Her gaze shifted beyond Benoit's shoulder as Hamish appeared in the doorway. "You are fired, Hamish."

The man gaped, then slowly closed his mouth and nodded. "Of course, my lady."

"You cannot fire the man for admiring my horse, my lady."

Her gaze snapped back to Benoit. "I can do

whatever I please within *my* home in regards to *my* servants. It is Hamish's duty to see that miscreants such as yourself do not darken my doorway. He failed, and I am well within my rights to terminate him for said failure of duty."

The miscreant moved closer. "And what of me? If I fail to perform my duty to your exacting standards, will I be terminated?"

"Have you forgotten you declined my offer of payment? You will not be in my employ if you are not paid, *monsieur*, therefore I will be in no position to terminate you."

"I wonder…" He set his hat on the table and reached toward her. She leaned back but failed to avoid the brush of his leather clad index finger along her cheek. "Have you planned and calculated exactly what position you will be in?"

Eirene sucked in a breath as heat flooded her face. "It is too early in the morning for inappropriate innuendos, *monsieur*. You have my permission to take your leave."

His gaze, which had been tracking the infuriating glide of his finger along her cheekbone, lifted. "I did not ask for your permission, my lady, so I believe I will stay a moment longer so that I might do this."

He kissed her. In the breakfast room, in full view of the street-facing window and the open door at his back. Surely, this was uncommonly bold behavior even for a rake. In fact, why was the man even awake at such an early hour?

The pressure of his mouth lessened. "You could kiss me back, my lady."

"Why?"

He smiled. Against her lips. What a truly singular sensation to experience.

To Eirene's surprise, he straightened and took a step back. "Forgive my intrusion this morning, my lady. I do hope the rest of your day goes as planned."

She could only stare as he bowed and left the room. After a few moments, she hurried to the window and caught sight of him riding away. The riderless horse trotted obediently alongside, attached to Benoit's saddle by a lead. She watched until she could no longer see him, then stepped back from the window and lightly touched her lips. Why had he kissed her again?

"My lady?"

She turned to find Hamish hovering in the doorway. "Wipe that downtrodden look off your face, Hamish. You are not fired." As if she could manage without the man. Besides, he was guilty of nothing more than admiring a fine looking beast belonging to a fine looking man.

Heavens. What was wrong with her? Next, she would be composing poetry about Benoit's thighs— eyes! Gracious. As if she had looked at the man's thighs as they cradled the side of his mount. No lady would ever behave in such a fashion, especially one determined to live out her life devoid of male companionship.

"His lordship left without his coat again, my lady."

Eirene noticed the coat folded over Hamish's forearm. She was tempted to have it burned so Benoit would have no further excuse to arrive unannounced at her door. "I will have a message in need of being delivered to his lordship later today. You may send the coat along with it."

She would also send out the cancellation notices to the other candidates. She no longer believed Benoit might change his mind. After all, he had come to her this morning to make an attempt to douse any damage done by the article. And she had behaved horribly in response.

Perhaps she *was* a bit too prickly. Or perhaps Benoit simply roused her less admirable character traits. He had accused her of doing the same. Perhaps they were simply two people incapable of rubbing along in harmony with one another.

Hamish cleared his throat. "Will that be all, my lady?"

She waved him away, still distracted by her thoughts. Why kiss her if he found her so offensive? It made no sense, though, men generally did not make sense. She really should not spend another moment thinking about the man.

Eirene poured a fresh cup of tea and carried it down the corridor to her study. Throwing open the curtains to allow the morning sun to filter in, she took a seat behind her desk and reached for a clean sheet of paper and her pen. With a bit more force than necessary, she dipped the pen into the ink, then scratched out the first of four cancellation messages. Once that task was complete, she moved on to a much more important matter. That of outlining for the monsieur the details of their rendezvous, as he wished to call it.

After careful deliberation, she had decided upon Lady Palmer's ball. Originally, she had chosen a different event, one complete with the wished for chaise lounge, but eliminating the other candidates and seeing the article in the morning paper had convinced her to shift her timeframe forward. The sooner she saw to her ruination, the sooner she could quit London and return to the country.

She dipped her pen again. Lady Palmer's ball was rumored to be *the* crush of the season. Everyone would be in attendance to enjoy Lady Palmer's infamous hospitality as well as her unique art collection, which was located in a special gallery. Said gallery would provide the location for Eirene's ruination. The ball was tomorrow night. She acknowledged the lack of notice, but the monsieur likely planned to attend the ball already, so surely he could take a moment out of his evening to meet her in the gallery and…

Eirene lifted her gaze from the paper and stared unseeing across the room. The man would likely kiss her. *Again.* The thought drew her gaze to the list she had made following the man's abrupt departure the previous evening. She pulled it closer.

As per usual, she had split the paper in half in order to illustrate the pros and cons of the current dilemma, that being her decision to choose Benoit to see to her ruination. She had been quite prepared to change her mind if the cons had outweighed the pros, but in the end, the two columns had ended up being identical. The list she now held was the third one she had comprised. The first two had gone into the fire. The outcome had remained the same each time.

For every pro in favor of Benoit was also a con.
Pro: He is no gentleman.
Con: He is no gentleman.
Pro: He is distractingly handsome.
Con: He is distractingly handsome.

Pro: He kissed me.
Con: He kissed me.
Pro: I liked his kiss.
Con: I liked his kiss.

Eirene crumpled the list and threw it across the desk in the direction of the fire. It fell well short, of course, but it did not matter. Burning the evidence would change nothing. She could no longer pretend to find the man objectionable, nor could she pretend to have not spent the entire night lying awake in bed reliving their kiss.

Despite the brevity of said kiss, it had been long enough to alert her to one very important truth; she would not walk away from The Scheme unscathed. Allowing Benoit to do what had to be done in order to ruin her, she would have to allow much more than a fleeting kiss. He would have to put his hands upon her person. Upon her bare flesh.

She sat back in her chair and pressed a hand to the fichu tucked inside her bodice. Her nipples puckered at the memory of Benoit sliding a very similar fichu from her bodice. The sensation had left her feeling burned. In fact, much about the man had left her feeling overheated. His mouth on her neck had made her feel feverish. His lips on hers had nearly caused her to perspire. The sight of his collarbone…

Eirene cut the memory short and waved a hand in front of her face to cool the air. Tomorrow evening, once inside Lady Palmer's gallery, she would see a great deal more than Benoit's collarbone.

God willing, the experience would not turn her into a pile of ash.

Chapter Six

Adrien refolded the letter from Lady Rowe-Weston, which had just been handed to him by the club's doorman. Not surprisingly, the lady had outlined the details of their rendezvous with the exacting attention of a military general planning a campaign. He could not help but smile as he tucked the letter into his waistcoat.

Part of him was tempted to reply with his own planned strategy. A strategy that would begin with a kiss that lasted longer than a fleeting moment before progressing into much deeper, more intimate terrain. Such as his hands upon her luscious curves and her hands upon any part of his person she desired to touch. He had accused her of being prickly, and he was determined to soothe her thorns before their rendezvous concluded.

"Devil take you, Benoit." Samuel Petley appeared at Adrien's table without warning, hissing the curse through clenched teeth so as not to draw attention.

Adrien sat back in his chair and gazed up at Cyril's cousin. "Care to elaborate, Petley?"

Petley took the vacant seat across the table, his movements sharp with poorly restrained anger. He narrowed his dark eyes and leaned forward. "Is it true?"

"I do not read minds, Petley. Is what true?" Though Adrien suspected he knew the motivation behind

Petley's appearance and anger.

"That not so subtle *on dit* in this morning's paper. Am I correct in assuming you were the 'dashing Vicomte seen exiting Lady Rowe-Weston's home'?"

"I do not see how it concerns you one way or the other."

If possible, the man's eyes grew darker than their natural coal black coloring. "It concerns me, you imbecile, because I intend to marry the woman."

"From what I have heard, the *lady* will not have you." And considering the burning intent in Petley's dark gaze, Adrien vowed to do whatever necessary to keep the cad far away from Lady Rowe-Weston. Hell, he would marry the woman himself if— *Whoa!* Where had that ridiculous thought come from?

"What difference does that make?" Spoken like a true scoundrel.

Adrien uncrossed his legs under the table in order to lean forward. He pitched his voice low so as not to be overheard by nearby gentlemen. "That sounded an awful lot like a threat."

Petley's eyes narrowed. "Why could you not have bowed out gracefully as I requested? Why must you make this a competition between us?"

"You assume there is a competition, Petley."

Before Petley could reply, a waiter appeared at the table. "This came for you, my lord." Petley snatched the folded missive from the man's gloved hand. His expression tightened as he read the contents, and Adrien actually sat back when Petley shifted his gaze across the table.

"Damn you to hell, Benoit."

"Let me guess. Lady Rowe-Weston no longer begs

the pleasure of your—"

"I have tried my damnedest to have a meeting with that woman," Petley hissed, while balling up the paper. "Now, because of you, my best chance has been cancelled."

Adrien gestured toward the crinkled note clutched in Sam's fist. "You cannot blame me for the whims of a lady. I did nothing to convince her to cancel your appointment."

"You are lying, Benoit." Petley stood with a loud screech of his chair that drew several curious glances. "In fact, lying is what you do best, is it not?"

Adrien stood as well. "What are you implying, Petley?" There was no way for Petley to know Adrien's secret. Was there?

Petley threw the balled up paper toward Adrien. It hit his chest and bounced to the table. It was a rather childish act, but it managed to illicit a few shocked gasps from those watching the growing confrontation. No doubt someone would liken it to a glove across the face, but Adrien refused to be baited.

"If you have something to say to me, Petley, be a man and say it."

"Stay away from Lady Rowe-Weston, Benoit. I am warning you, as a friend, things will get quite unpleasant if you do not." Petley stalked away before Adrien could respond.

Adrien remained standing after Sam's departure. He soon became aware of the many sets of eyes watching him. Wonderful, no doubt the rumor mill would be all atwitter with reports of his near fisticuffs with Lord Petley. Well, Cyril had said something would happen to divert the gossips from Adrien's visit to Lady

Rowe-Weston's house, had he not? Speaking of Cyril. It seemed his friend had some explaining to do if Adrien correctly interpreted Sam's threat.

Nodding to the gentlemen nearest him, Adrien took his leave, determined to find Cyril and get some answers before meeting Lady Rowe-Weston tomorrow evening at Lady Palmer's ball.

****

Having had no success locating Cyril the previous evening, Adrien was left with no choice but to rise early and ambush his friend over breakfast.

Before launching his attack, he eyed the half eaten slice of toast placed before Cyril. "Are you unwell, *mon ami*?"

Cyril glanced up, eyes bright, cheeks rosy. "Unwell? Me? No. I've never felt better." He waved Adrien into the room, then stabbed at the paper with his index finger. "It seems I was correct about the gossips finding a new morsel to sink their fangs into."

"Let me guess," Adrien drawled on his way to the side board, "my confrontation with your cousin."

"Indeed. Care to tell me the actual story?"

In no mood to eat, Adrien carried his coffee cup and the pot to the table. Sitting down, he reached for the paper to see for himself how the gossips had interpreted his *tête-à-tête* with Sam. No doubt the embellishments would be worthy of a lurid novel.

Dearest Reader,

It seems there was quite the row between a certain dashing Vicomte and Lord P. Rumor has it the argument revolved around a certain Lady of Grand Wealth and nearly escalated into pistols at dawn. It is common knowledge that Lord P wishes to marry the

Lady of Great Wealth, and now we must wonder if our dashing Vicomte shares the same goal. It should be noted, said Vicomte was once more seen in the vicinity of said lady's home, in possession of two horses and a rather disappointed countenance.

Has the lady rejected her French suitor? I vow to flush out the details, dearest readers...

"It is mostly accurate." He could not help but wonder what Lady Rowe-Weston would think if she saw the piece. Two appearances in the gossip section in as many mornings. It was advantageous Lady Palmer's ball was that evening, or the gossips might succeed in the task of ruining Lady Rowe-Weston's reputation before Adrien could.

"What *actually* occurred?"

Adrien propped his elbows on the table and cradled his cup in both hands. "Sam took offense to yesterday's gossip about Lady Rowe-Weston and myself. He reiterated his intent to marry her. Things took a nasty turn when he received a letter from the lady cancelling their appointment. He blamed me for the lost opportunity to finally gain entrance to the lady's private sanctum, then said some rather interesting things in regards to my ability to lie."

"Oh? Whatever could he have been alluding to?"

Adrien did not answer. He simply stared at Cyril over the rim of his coffee cup and waited. Cyril was an incredibly intelligent individual. It would not take long for him to piece things together. Adrien knew the moment Cyril did so. The bushy, brown brows flew up, his mouth fell open, and his cheeks grew redder.

Adrien saluted Cyril with his cup. "How did Sam learn of my true identity?"

"You cannot believe I told him?" Cyril shook his head with enough force to challenge the hold of his pomade. "I would never betray you, Adrien."

"And yet, I never told anyone but you."

"You told Lady Rowe-Weston."

Adrien employed another steady, silent stare in response to Cyril's ludicrous suggestion that Lady Rowe-Weston had somehow transferred that knowledge to Sam.

Cyril visibly deflated. "The entire family knew."

Very slowly, Adrien set his cup upon the table. "Knew? As in from the very beginning?" And no one had ever said a word to him? Why? Why allow him to keep up such a farce?

Cyril nodded. "Yes. Sam's mother is Adrien Benoit's aunt."

Well then. Adrien's hands began to shake as shock rolled through him.

"The Petleys and Benoits go way back," Cyril went on, clearly content to oversimplify the matter. "My grandfather was—"

Adrien looked up from his hands as Cyril ceased talking. "What?"

"You are awfully pale of a sudden, Adrien. Are you quite all right?"

"No." He shook his head then leaned back in his chair. "Why did your parents never tell me they knew? Why allow me to go about behaving as though I outranked them?"

"You might believe you behaved in that fashion, but you did not. As for them telling you they knew, what did it matter? They loved you like a son. Nothing would have changed that."

He knew Cyril spoke the truth about Sir and Lady Petley feelings for him. No one could replace the parents he had lost in France, but the Petleys had come close. They had treated him as though he and Cyril were brothers, as though he had always been a part of their family, and always would be. It should not matter to him that they allowed him to believe the farce of his identity had to be maintained. But it did matter. He had lived a lie under their roof when he could have simply been himself.

He glanced at Cyril. "It would have been nice to know the love and affection they offered was for a blacksmith's son and not a marquis'." And there it was. He had not known they loved him for *him*.

"If they were alive today they—"

"Don't. Please." A moment of silence fell between them as Adrien gathered his thoughts and emotions and Cyril patiently waited. "Why did Sam's parents not take me in? Why did it fall to your father?"

"Sam's parents did not have the money to support another."

Jesu. The salvos were never ending.

"No money? Sam is many things, but poor is not one of them."

"Actually, Sam is quite poor. Every pound he wins at the tables or at the track is immediately dumped into the estate, and with his father not long for this world, he has grown desperate to rebuild the family coffers before he inherits so he might be in a better position to provide for his mother and…sister."

Adrien did not miss the slight hesitation in Cyril's longwinded explanation. "Cyril, if there is something else, tell me now. I want no more secrets between us."

Cyril averted his gaze. "Jillian is not Sam's sister. She is his daughter."

Adrien allowed that nugget to sink in. "Illegitimate, I presume?"

He pictured the girl, not an easy task, given he'd only laid eyes upon her one time. From what he could recall, she was short of stature, lithe, as dark in coloring as Sam and with features lovely enough to lure many a suitor to her door when the time was right.

"Yes, the by blow of one of Sam's many mistresses, though only Sam's mother is aware of the truth. It is my understanding that Lady Petley—"

Adrien held up his hands in surrender. "No. Do not waste your breath or my time attempting to explain the ins and outs of that particular arrangement. Whether or not Sam has a daughter is no concern of mine." Discovering Sam was in need of funds, however, was very concerning. No wonder the man was so hungry to marry Lady Rowe-Weston.

"Jillian's true parentage should concern you, Adrien, because with that bit of knowledge I've just handed you the leverage you need if Sam decides to expose you."

"Do you believe he would stoop so low?"

Cyril shook his head while reaching for the sliver of toast. "I will speak to him, but no, I do not believe the threat holds any weight. As you said, Sam in many things, but he is not stupid. He cannot afford a scandal of any kind, not if he hopes to launch Jillian next year."

"I do hope you are right about your cousin, Cyril. I really do." Not just for his own sake, but for Lady Rowe-Weston's. Cyril had not seen the look in Sam's eyes when the lady's name came up. There had been a level of darkness that lent a rather sinister cast to Sam's desperation to wed the woman. She would need to be warned.

Chapter Seven

Adrien stood toward the back of Lady Palmer's ballroom, sipping champagne while covertly awaiting Lady Rowe-Weston's arrival. Her message had instructed him to wait for her in the gallery, but he thought it best they be seen together beforehand. It was always good to stir the pot before serving the feast.

Good lord, had anyone ever said such an idiotic thing?

Shaking his head, he focused on the warm champagne in his hand.

"Benoit." Henry Westhaven cut a path through the growing crowd to join Adrien at his chosen pillar. He, too, carried a flute of champagne. "Why are you hiding back here?" Planting a shoulder against the pillar, Westhaven surveyed the guests, no doubt on the hunt for a certain Miss Parish.

"How are things progressing with Miss Parish?"

Henry flicked his brown gaze toward Adrien. "The woman is more stubborn than a thirty year old mule."

Adrien smiled into his champagne. Clearly, Miss Parish had not accepted Westhaven's overtures toward her, assuming the lad had made any. Westhaven was not what one would call aggressive when it came to courting Miss Parish. Hell, the woman likely did not even know Westhaven fancied her.

"You keep staring toward the stairs," Westhaven

remarked. "Who are you waiting for?"

"Must I be waiting for anyone?"

"Yes."

Damn Westhaven and his uncanny instincts. "If I tell you, you must not breathe a word to anyone, not even Kilby."

Henry's eyes flashed with curiosity. "And if I do?"

"I will see that Miss Parish knows the difference between an English and a French kiss."

Henry's gaze narrowed. "Touch her and die, Benoit."

Adrien saluted with his champagne flute. "Good. We have an understanding then. I am waiting for Lady Rowe-Weston." As he said the words, the footman at the top of the stairs announced the lady's arrival. All heads swiveled, his and Henry's included.

She was a vision.

"My God, *that* is Lady Rowe-Weston?"

"*Oui.*" Adrien answered without taking his eyes off her. Hell, Napoleon could have strolled into the ballroom, and he still would not have been able to tear his gaze away. She wore gold. Like a goddess. Her dark auburn hair was swept up in an intricate display of coils and curls. The arrangement looked heavy, but one would never know it by the confident angle of the lady's chin. As if she dared those staring at her to find fault. How could anyone?

Her gown was flawless. A pale gold sheath accented across the bodice, sleeves, and hem with deep, rich gold embroidery. The cut was much more modest than some worn by the other female guests, hiding more bosom than it exposed, but he still stared. On the two occasions he had been in the lady's presence, her gowns had been sensible and lacking in any feature that might awaken a man's lust. Funny how a bit of bosom could throw a match on one's libido.

Jesu, if looking at her set him ablaze, touching her would likely incinerate him.

"She is breathtaking in a rather nontraditional way," Westhaven commented. "Are those freckles?"

Adrien did not answer. He shoved his champagne flute into Henry's empty hand, then stalked off without excusing himself. The crowd, distracted by Lady Rowe-Weston's arrival and likely her nontraditional beauty, shifted out of his way as if controlled by an unseen force. None of them seemed to notice him until he had mounted the stairs and offered his arm.

Lady Rowe-Weston stared at his crooked arm, then at his face. "This was not the plan."

"Some plans require slight alterations, my lady."

She continued to hesitate. The crowd began to murmur.

"Do you mean to cause two scenes this evening, my lady?"

"Of course not." She coiled her gloved fingers around his elbow.

****

Eirene attempted not to grip Benoit's arm too tightly lest he ascertain the depths of her discomfort. Not that she would admit it, but her relief over his appearance at her side had nearly dropped her to her knees. She had not anticipated how it would feel to have hundreds of eyes staring at her. Nor had she planned for the self-doubt those gazes had provoked. She had been questioning everything—her gown, her hairstyle, the decision not to powder her freckles. But then Benoit had appeared to offer his arm and a seductive smile.

Her initial scold had been a way to disguise her true reaction. She had not allowed herself to imagine him in evening wear, and the reality stole her breath. Had he any idea how glorious he looked with his pale hair loose, its tips brushing the shoulders of his black evening coat? It appeared not a drop of pomade had been applied to those waves. They begged to be touched.

She curled the fingers of her free hand into a fist. *Petting* Monsieur Benoit was not part of her plan for the evening.

"I will escort you to Lady Palmer, then take my leave."

Eirene glanced up at Benoit's profile, paying no mind to those who attempted to press close for an introduction. "I imagine I could have managed to locate the woman on my own."

He shook his head without looking at her. "As I said, it is better for us to be seen together, to add fuel to the fire laid by the gossips."

Ah, yes, the gossips. The piece in the morning paper had turned her breakfast to dust upon her tongue. How dare Benoit and Petley argue over her, as if she were some sort of buried treasure to be awarded to the first man to find the X.

"Do you imagine Petley is in attendance?" Not knowing what the man looked like, she had no way of ascertaining the answer for herself.

"I have not seen him." Benoit suddenly halted and turned to face Eirene. "There is something you should know in regards to Petley, my lady." He kept his voice

she did not look away. One simply did not give the cut direct to a woman of Eirene's wealth, no matter what one thought of her.

Eirene smiled. The woman did not. Well, so much for that attempt at kindness. Turning her back on the woman, she gathered her skirts and stepped out onto the terrace, a lovely stone getaway well within sight and sound of the crow-like chaperones. Eirene moved all the way to the railing and braced her hands upon the smooth stone. The garden below was not large, but it glowed beautifully in the moonless night as a result of the dozens upon dozens of lanterns scattered about. A few couples moved in and out of the illumination.

Watching the couples meander, as if they possessed not a care in the world, she sighed.

"It seems a bit early in the evening to already possess regrets about your first foray into Society."

Eirene kept her hands atop the rail but turned her head in the direction of the masculine voice. A man stood cloaked in the shadows caused by the overhang of a small balcony. The burning end of his cigar allowed her to find him.

"I did not come out here to engage in conversation, sir, especially with a man who chooses to hide from a lady."

He tossed his cigar aside, then stepped out from under the balcony and into the light that spilled from within the ballroom. "Will you converse now that I no longer hide?"

"I will not." Eirene turned away, casting her attention out over the garden and away from the tall, dark, and handsome scoundrel to her right. "We have not been introduced, sir."

"Technically," he drawled, coming closer, "*you* were the first to breach social etiquette, my lady."

Eirene whipped her head back around. "Pardon me? I did no such thing, sir. I merely chose to step out onto this terrace to find a bit of fresh—"

"You invited me to a private meeting in your home."

She snapped her mouth closed. Odd, while in the midst of planning for this evening, she had not once considered encountering any of the other candidates. Her thoughts had been entirely focused upon Benoit and whether or not he would actually do what he had promised. It was not like her to be so unprepared or to overlook something so very obvious. Of course, the other candidates would attend Lady Palmer's ball. Such an event offered endless opportunities for such men to misbehave. Looking at the man before her, she attempted to ascertain which of the candidates he might be based upon his looks and what she had read about each man.

Tall. Dark. Handsome in a boyish, eager spaniel sort of way. Fine form. Excellent tailoring. A taste for fine cigars. Ah, yes. Westhaven. Proud to have not lost her facility for deduction, she managed a tight smile. "A gentleman would never remark upon such a thing, Mister Westhaven."

His brown eyes widened. "Color me impressed and a tad envious, my lady, that you would know me on sight, but I never would have guessed you were the reclusive Lady Rowe-Weston."

"You are written about rather extensively, Mister Westhaven. One need only pay attention to gain the information needed to recognize you in person."

"So I am, in the flesh, precisely how they paint me to be in the papers?"

She refused to react to his cheeky choice of words. "Yes."

It was true. The gossips had done a much better job describing Mister Westhaven than they had Benoit. She need not worry about any surprising discoveries, such as eyes that changed from deep pewter to molten silver or a voice like honey that carried a faint flavor of France or a collarbone tempting enough to recall the sight of while trying to sleep.

No. Mister Westhaven was precisely how she imagined him to be. And he would have made a horrible choice. Looks and charm, notwithstanding.

"Might I ask you a personal question, my lady?"

"That depends."

He smiled in a way that slowly spread his wide, sensual lips, crinkled the bridge of his nose, and narrowed his eyes. It was a wonder there were not debutantes attached to the man's silk-clad ankles. Benoit's tidbit of information about Westhaven filtered into her thoughts. The man was madly in love, according to Benoit. Was that his reason for hiding in the shadows? Was the object of his affection due to arrive, or worse, enjoying herself with another?

"You may ask one personal question, Mister Westhaven, if I can do the same."

He arched a brow, then nodded. "Very well. I have nothing to hide."

Eirene turned to prop a hip against the rail and cross her arms. "Go on then."

He eyed her stance with an openly amused gaze. "Why did you invite me into your home for a private meeting?"

She should have anticipated that would be the question. And yet, she had not and was therefore unprepared. Again. "The matter has been attended—"

"By Benoit, I presume?"

"Well, after a fashion, yes."

"The man could not keep his eyes off you when you entered the ballroom. I do not imagine I am the only one to notice."

His words should have concerned her, but instead, she felt nothing but a slow, rising heat. It began low in her belly then spread outward. "I cannot control Benoit's actions."

"Do you wish to?"

"That is two questions, Mister Westhaven, and you only asked permission to voice one. It is my turn." He conceded with a nod. "Why were you hiding in the shadows? And do not claim you were not. We are two intelligent adults well versed on the definition of hiding."

"I was sulking."

"Sulking?" Hardly the activity she would expect a gentleman rogue to admit to.

"Yes. Moments before deciding to duck out here and hide, I learned a certain young lady will not be present this evening."

"Ah." Eirene nodded. The object of his affection had changed her mind. "I have no experience with unrequited love, Mister Westhaven, but I can easily imagine how uncomfortable it must be. Not to mention fraught with disappointments and empty expectations. I hope you do not allow this young lady to steal the best years of your life away while you wait upon a return of affection she might never offer."

He stared at her, as if she had sprouted a forked tongue and fangs. "Forgive me, my lady, but you speak as though privy to details you have no knowledge of."

"Benoit mentioned you were madly in love."

"Did he?" Westhaven drew back, then shot an angry glance out across the garden. "Benoit should learn to hold his tongue."

"He meant no harm, and truth be told, I rather forced him to tell me."

Westhaven returned his gaze to her. "Dare I ask?"

"Of course. As part of my meeting with him, I asked that he give his opinion of the other candidates' suitability, and he rendered you unsuitable based on the fact you are madly in love."

"Suitable for what?"

She stared at him until he seemed to realize she would not answer. "Benoit did not mention the young lady's name if that helps put your mind at ease."

"How generous of him."

"Yes, well, at any rate. It has been lovely meeting you, Mister Westhaven. I wish you great success in your pursuits and bid you good evening." She gathered her skirts to step away from the railing, but Westhaven moved to block her retreat.

"You are a most unusual woman, my lady."

"Is that meant to be a compliment?"

He shook his head. "Perceive it more as a warning."

A chill washed over her skin, extinguishing any lingering heat from his earlier mention of Benoit. "A warning? I fear you have lost me, Mister Westhaven."

"When I received your cancellation message, I

experienced only a brief moment of dismay, followed by mild curiosity, followed by amusement. There are others who might not have reacted the same. Surely, you read this morning's paper?"

"You speak of the near fisticuffs between Benoit and Petley. As I said, I cannot control Benoit—"

"It is not Benoit you should worry about." He looked over his shoulder as the sound of approaching voices drifted toward them. In moments, their false privacy would be shattered. He met her gaze while bowing over her knuckles. "It has been a pleasure, my lady." He lingered over the gesture. "Do be careful now that you have joined Society. Not all gentlemen deserve the moniker."

Eirene stared after Westhaven as he stalked across the terrace to descend the stairs, which led to a lower terrace and eventually the garden. His parting words echoed in her mind, leaving her with a new urgency to see the evening finished and her carriages packed for a return to the country. She had no desire to risk a meeting with Lord Petley. Her best strategy against that particular gentleman's unwanted attentions was avoidance, meaning she would do best not to return to the ballroom. Surely, the garden would offer another way into the mansion.

Lifting her skirts, she went the way of Westhaven, determined to bypass Society, find the gallery, make use of Benoit's promised services, then call it a night. By this time tomorrow, she should be well on her way *home*.

Chapter Eight

After a ridiculous amount of time spent looking for a gallery, which clearly existed alongside Avalon or some other mythical place, Eirene decided to admit defeat. With her hair sagging in its pins, her gown clinging to her in uncomfortably damp places, and her patience long lost, she traversed a narrow corridor for the third time and stepped into the dark solitude of a room she had passed during her failed search. The interior smelled of wood smoke and leather, reminding her of her grandfather. They were the scents that had followed him throughout his day, trailing in his wake or lingering after his departure. She inhaled deeply and instantly felt better.

"Bonjour."

Eirene made herself dizzy as she spun toward the French greeting. "Benoit?"

It had best be him because she simply would not forgive herself for *twice* being in a situation with a strange man hiding in the shadows.

"Do you know any other Frenchman who might be waiting for you in a dark room?"

"You are supposed to be waiting for me in the gallery." Though she doubted even Sir Francis Drake could locate said gallery.

"Had I done as instructed, you would now be in this room alone."

A light flared, causing her to blink at the sudden brightness. When she regained her vision, it was to the sight of Benoit propped on the edge of a small desk. She could not help but wonder if men graced with such looks practiced such poses. It seemed ridiculous to imagine Benoit watching himself in a mirror as he arranged himself on various pieces of furniture, but how else explain the uncanny knack he possessed to always present himself in a way she found captivating?

She pulled her gaze away from the sight of his silk-clad calf, showcased to perfection as it was against the darkness of the desk front. "I do not believe Lady Palmer possesses a gallery."

"It is located in the garden, within the skeleton of a rather fanciful folly, from what I hear. Impossible to locate unless one is given directions."

Why the devil had no one told her that bit of useful information? It had been Hamish who had suggested Lady Palmer's ball, and when asked to explain the choice, he had mentioned the popularity of the lady's art gallery. Would it have pained him to mention the gallery was not located *within* the house? As for Lady Palmer, why have an art gallery outside? Why expose an art collection to the elements? What sane individual would do such a thing?

She recalled Lady Palmer's fluttering headdress of peacock feathers and reassessed her use of the word sane.

"As fascinating as it is to watch you think, there is a rather important matter in need of discussion." Benoit's words drew Eirene's focus back toward him, the picture he presented, and the reason behind the entire evening.

Turning back to the door, she pushed it closed but did not latch it. If her fingers shook as they released the knob, she pretended not to notice. After a deep breath, she faced Benoit. "All right then."

She allowed her gaze to take in the rest of the room. It was a small space, boasting only a modest hearth, the desk beneath Benoit's hip, a chair for whomever wished to occupy the desk, and a settee angled to benefit from the fire's warmth. She frowned at the settee. Its upholstery sagged in the center, hinting at cushions no longer capable of providing comfort.

"It's a rather sad space, is it not?" Benoit remarked from his perch upon the desk. "Especially considering the grandeur of the rest of the place. One has to wonder who uses this room. Certainly not Lady Palmer. I assume you met the woman?"

Eirene nodded but continued to eye the settee. Would the two of them even fit? Lying down seemed out of the question.

"Then you will agree she is more likely to decorate a room with a bit more *joie de vive*."

"Of course." What had he said? She found it difficult to listen while trying to reason out the positioning of her ruination. Perhaps if Benoit sat upon the settee, and she—

"People have managed to fornicate upon much less." He spoke directly in her ear, causing her to nearly jump into his arms. Smiling, he grasped her upper arms lightly until she had regained stability. "You are looking at that poor settee as though it is a bed of nails."

Eirene lifted her chin despite the heat flaring in her face. "I will trust your experience on such matters, *monsieur*. It is, after all, why I hired you."

"Of course, but before I prove to you just how accommodating such a piece of furniture can be, there is something you need to know."

Eirene stepped back from Benoit and began peeling off her long gloves. "Go on. I am listening."

"Petley is quite determined to marry you, whether you wish it or not."

Stopping with the second glove half off, Eirene stared at Benoit. "You make it sound as if the man plans to throw a sack over my head and drag me to Gretna Green?"

"I would not put it past him."

She laughed. "Do not be ridiculous. Such things only happen in horrid novels. Lord Petley is a gentleman set to inherit a respectable title. He has a younger sister due to launch next season and a family name untarnished by past scandals. Why would you believe, for even a moment, he would do anything to threaten his future or that of his sister?"

"I was wrong when I told you he did not need your money." The seriousness of Benoit's tone opened the door to a trickle of doubt within Eirene. "His family is horribly in debt. The estate is close to ruin. If he does not marry well, he will not be able to launch his sister as anything but a desperate debutante in need of a fortune."

"I see." Eirene returned her attention to the glove and finished removing it. She folded it over the other, then brushed past Benoit to set them atop the desk. She stared at them while considering Benoit's revelation. "If what you say about Petley is true—" She tossed a quick glance over her shoulder. "—and I have no reason to doubt you, considering you are not the first to issue a warning this evening, then it is more than fortuitous that after tonight I will be considered ruined goods. A man with Petley's reputation will not wish to take a tarnished woman as wife."

She waited for Benoit to agree, but he did not.

"Who issued the first warning?"

"Mister Westhaven."

His gaze darkened. "You encountered Westhaven?"

"On the terrace, yes. He was sulking over the absence of his—"

"I do not care why Westhaven was sulking. Did he act the gentleman with you?"

"He was all that would be considered charming and mannerly. Though he was rather put out upon learning you told me he is in love."

"He will recover. What did he say about Petley?"

"Nothing as specific as what you have laid out, just a warning to remember not all gentlemen *are* gentlemen."

"I wish I could predict what Petley will or will not do."

Eirene made a dismissive gesture. "I appreciate your concern, *monsieur*, but after tonight, I plan to quit London and return to the solitude of the country. My trunks are already packed, so you have my permission to think no more on the matter. Besides, I find it hard to imagine Petley's desperation would cause him to forgo the rest of the season in order to chase after me. I am hardly the only wealthy, unmarried woman in all of England." She saw from Benoit's tight expression that, despite wishing to, he could not argue her logic. "Now then, shall we commence with my ruination?"

Unsure what else to do, Eirene moved to the settee and perched upon the edge of the sagging cushion. The item proved as uncomfortable as it looked. Back straight, hands folded in her lap, she waited for Benoit to do whatever it was men did in such situations. She imagined he would begin by removing some of his clothing.

Her gaze strayed toward his cravat. Did the situation allow for her to ask him to remove *specific* articles of clothing? Weren't the rules of this false seduction hers to make? Yes. She rather believed they were.

"I would like you to remove your cravat, *monsieur*." There. That had not been too difficult, and it had proved only mildly uncomfortable.

He made no move to obey. "Is that how this is going to go? You bark an order. I obey."

"That seems the most efficient way to go about things, does it not?"

"Efficiency does not belong in a seduction, my lady."

"This is not a real seduction, *monsieur*." It would grow tedious if she had to continuously remind him of that fact.

"It might not be a real seduction," he admitted while moving closer to the settee, "but there will be nothing false about the feel of my hands on your person."

Well!

Eirene shifted in an attempt to ease a sudden bout of discomfort followed by a feeling of moistness. Had the cushion been damp when she sat down? Mortified to have overlooked the possibility, she shot to her feet and spun around to study the upholstery. The cushion revealed nothing save for the slight depression of her recent occupation.

"Did it suddenly occur to you the fabric might have fleas?"

She twisted to look at Benoit. "It felt moist." Her words caused him to bite his lower lip in an obvious attempt not to laugh. "Why is that amusing?"

He shook his head. "I refuse to answer that."

"Clearly you also refuse to remove your cravat."

"Ask nicely."

She rolled her eyes. "Will you *please* remove your cravat, Monsieur Benoit?"

He lifted his hands and began pulling at the knot. "In private you can refer to me as Monsieur Cloutier. Or Adrien, if you prefer." The knot came undone, and he allowed the crinkled ends of fabric to hang loose. "I assume you wish to have me do this as well?" He unfastened his collar before she could reply and splayed open the fabric.

Ah, there it was. The collarbone that had haunted her nights. Once more, it attracted her gaze as if it held the secrets to life's most vexing puzzles.

"What is your given name, my lady?"

"Eirene," she answered without thought. "As in the Greek goddess of peace."

"You dressed accordingly for the bearer of such a name."

She dragged her gaze to his eyes. "Pardon me?"

He gestured toward her gown. "I thought you a goddess when you appeared at the top of the stairs."

"You are attempting to woo me again, *monsieur*."

"My apologies." He did not sound sorry.

"I imagine you would be more comfortable without your jacket, *monsieur*."

"Considering you did not word that as a command…" He shrugged out of the garment. His movements pulled at his open collar, and she stared at the base of his throat, as if it were an oasis in a very hot desert. He carelessly tossed the jacket across the desk.

Eirene licked her parched lips. "There." She cleared her dry throat. "Is that not more comfortable?"

"Come here, Eirene."

She snapped her gaze to his. "Did I give you permission to use my name?" Though the sound of it wrapped in his honey voice just might replace her dreams about his collarbone.

He held out his hand. "Come here, Eirene."

"Why?"

"Because I cannot ruin you from across the room."

"But the settee is—"

"We will get to the settee in time." He extended his hand. "Come."

Eirene accepted his outstretched hand. His fingers curled around hers, then he eased her toward him. Close enough to place their joined hands at the base of her spine. The position thrust her bosom against his chest. She used her other hand as a barrier, placing it flat over his heart and locking her arm so he could not pull her closer without using force.

He smiled down at her, the position of the desk lamp casting half his face in shadow while leaving the other half dominated by one gloriously silver eye. "Go on then. Touch it."

She shook her head, feigning misunderstanding

even while her gaze drifted toward his collarbone. Not only was she in a position to touch, she could kiss it if she wished. What would it be like to run her lips along that hard ridge?

Benoit's free hand covered the one she had braced against his chest. With ease, he guided it up toward his open collar then *inside* the parted fabric to place the tips of her fingers over his collarbone. She spread her fingers, and he released her hand, leaving her free to explore at will.

And explore she did.

Like a fascinated child petting their first pony, Eirene dragged her hand all the way to the curve of Benoit's shoulder, causing his shirt to pull against the still fastened buttons. Part of her was aware of him seeing to the matter, but only because the fabric loosened enough to allow her to curl her hand up over his shoulder. His skin radiated heat like a well-tended fire.

Without thinking. Without considering the whys or why nots, Eirene dipped her head and placed her lips against Benoit's collarbone. He shuddered beneath her touch. The shoulder muscles pressed to the underside of her wrist flexed. His breath fanned the loose tendrils of her coif. Taking note of such things added to her boldness. Parting her lips, she touched his flesh with her tongue.

****

Adrien dropped his head back and stared at the ceiling.

Eirene Rowe-Weston was attempting to kill him. There was no other explanation for her maddening behavior. The wet glide of her tongue weakened his knees and sent a hot rush of blood to his groin as though he were a lad barely out of short pants. For a man accustomed to the feel of a woman's tongue *elsewhere*, his reaction to Eirene licking his damn collarbone was nothing less than shocking. God help him if she decided to explore points farther south.

He'd go off like a damn cannon.

As it were, when her mouth reached the hollow of his throat and her tongue began a slow glide up toward his Adam's apple, he cursed the gods of yore for not gifting him with the patience of a saint. He could not take another moment of her questing lips.

Taking hold of her elegant coif, he dug his fingers in amongst the pins and pearls until he found her scalp. She gasped against the underside of his chin, her breath hot and moist. He tugged, and she came away with an open-mouthed rasp of shock. He looked down into her wide copper eyes, then farther, to the sheen of moisture on her lower lip and the exaggerated puffiness of the upper. It was too much for any man to tolerate.

"Mon Dieu, tu es magnifique." And she was the most magnificent creature he had ever laid eyes on. Still gripping the back of her head, he anchored her for the descent of his mouth. She exhaled as soon as his lips covered hers. She tasted of tea and mint, and it made him aware of the tepid champagne that likely flavored his own mouth. She did not seem to mind.

The hand she had curled over his shoulder rose to cling to his nape. She held on for dear life, as if his kiss were the only thing preventing her from drowning. Funny that. Considering he felt as if kissing her had knocked him head first into a typhoon. Blood roared in his ears and in his groin. His heart knocked against his chest in a painful staccato he hadn't felt since stepping foot onto that small English ship off the coast of Dieppe. That had been fear of the unknown. Fear of failing to reach safety. Kissing Eirene sparked an entirely different level of fear.

Fear of never kissing her again.

Her tongue snaked alongside his. He could not have said which of them had initiated the contact. Their mouths were one. Their breaths mingled until he breathed for her and she for him. He'd never felt anything like it. Her fingers pulled at the hair above his nape, and he could have sworn he *tasted* the desperation of her touch. Her fingers reached higher into his hair, and he thanked the stars he had worn it loose. Who would have thought the feel of a woman's hand on his scalp could be erotic? He had had his hair pulled and tugged by lovers in the past but never had he particularly enjoyed the feel.

Eirene did not pull or tug. She explored. Fingers spread wide, she burrowed through his hair until her palm lay flush against the back of his head. The possessiveness of her touch was staggering and not a single bit off putting. Had it been possible, he would have ripped his heart out and dropped it at her feet.

Jesu.

The thought brought the kiss to an abrupt end.

Recalling the purpose behind his presence at Lady Palmer's ball, Adrien corralled his wayward emotions, then released Eirene. "It might be time to adjourn to the settee, my lady."

She blinked at him, then darted her tongue out to taste the fullness of her upper lip. Adrien had to avert his gaze lest he snatch her back into his arms for another ravishing kiss.

"Yes, of course." Her breathy voice only added to his torment. She glanced toward the settee, a frown marring her perfect brow. "I must admit to doubting whether it is big enough—"

"It will do," he interjected while taking her by the hand and leading her the short distance from desk to settee. Without releasing her, he sat with his arse flush to the back of the cushion and his shoulder blades digging painfully into the maker's sad attempt at a decorative, carved, wooden camel-back. Bloody hell, the floor would be more comfortable. Ignoring the protests of his body, he gave Eirene's hand a light tug. "Sit on my lap."

To her credit, she only hesitated for a moment before angling herself to sit sideways upon his thighs. He stopped her with a hand pressed to her hip. "Astride."

"Oh." Her gaze flicked down to his lap. He sat with his feet planted and knees spread. No doubt a shocking sight given her lack of experience in such matters.

"I am firmly encased in my breeches, Eirene. There is no harm in you sitting upon my lap." Her gaze flew to his face, and he took note of the doubt. It seemed she was not so inexperienced that she did not recognize a cockstand when she saw one. "You must trust me."

As much as Adrien craved the feel of her draped across his lap with her womanly core riding the ridge in his breeches and her breasts taunting within the confines of her bodice, if she balked, he would put an end to this rendezvous. If, after that, she still wished to ruin her reputation, they would simply choose another time and place after she had had enough time to come to terms with all that her ruination involved.

She did not, however, balk.

Gathering her skirts, she swung a leg over his thighs and settled against his groin like a woman born to the saddle. It took him a moment to breathe, and when he finally could, the action shuddered through him with enough vibration to make Eirene's breasts tremble. God, give him strength.

"Am I hurting you?"

He shook his head, then unclenched his jaw lest she assume he lied. "You are fine." *Fine*. He should go directly to hell for using such an inane word to describe the feel of her perched upon his lap. The tension in her thigh muscles alone nearly stole his ability to recall his name.

She shifted a little to the left then to the right. Doing so fitted her core tight against his erection. He nearly bit his tongue in half silencing a moan of torturous pleasure.

"What do we do now?" The innocence in her voice belied the heat radiating from between her thighs.

Adrien gathered his wits and lightly clasped her waist. "Honestly, we need do nothing. Being discovered thus would certainly be enough to cause a scandal."

Given the drape of her skirts over his legs, no one would have been able to definitively say what had or had not been going on under the gold fabric. Given the lust for gossip among the *ton*, most would assume the worst and Eirene's reputation would be in shambles.

Mission accomplished.

Now if only someone would come through the door before he lost the ability to keep his hands, mouth, and other parts of his body to himself.

Chapter Nine

Eirene stared at the man sprawled beneath her. The feel of him between her thighs was rather spectacular but, strangely, it could not quite compete with the sight of him. He had dropped his head back to look her in the eyes, and the position created a work of art worthy of being cast in marble. Neck chorded with tension, jaw clenched, nostrils flared, tousled hair spilled over the settee's wooden back, eyes bright with... Well, she imagined they were bright with *lust*, given the hardness within the fall of his breeches. She had not missed the way his body responded to her attempt to find a more comfortable position.

A tiny devil whispered in her ear to wiggle some more, to maybe press her breasts against his chest as well. Where such thoughts came from, she had not a clue, but she could not deny the strength of the temptation, not while the taste of his kiss lingered on and *in* her mouth. He might claim they need not do more than appear engaged in an illicit embrace, but she found herself wanting more than mere appearances. What a waste it would be to have such a fine man all but at her mercy and not be able to recall the feel of his skin beneath her fingers or the feel of his fingers upon her skin.

No. She would not spend the rest of her days living with such a regret. It was one thing to wish never to marry, it was quite another to ignore a chance to make a lasting memory.

"I believe it would be best if we made it look a little more believable." While she spoke, she reached for the edge of her bodice. There was a narrow ribbon, hidden amongst the gold embroidery. Its purpose, to cinch the bodice tight across her bosom and enhance the appearance of her cleavage. She located the short, trailing ends of the ribbon and tugged. The material loosened as she exhaled, exposing a goodly amount of her short stays.

"That is not necessary." He covered her hands with his, then shook his head when she lifted her gaze. "Most ballroom assignations are conducted without the removal of one's clothing."

Eirene arched a brow. "Are you an expert on such things, *monsieur*?"

"Is that not why you secured my particular services?"

"An odd inquiry from the very man who claimed I should not believe all I have read about him."

"*Touché*, my lady, but it does not alter the fact you need not remove any clothing."

She held his gaze, allowing herself to marvel at the stormy depths of his eyes. "And if I wish to remove my clothing, *monsieur*?"

He did not respond right away. In fact, the silence threatened to become unsettling.

Driven to the edge of her patience, Eirene was the first to speak. "Adrien?"

He chuckled and shook his head. "*Now* you decide to call me something other than Benoit." Again, he shook his head. "You are determined to drive me mad, I fear."

She had no idea how to respond, nor did he really offer her the chance. Withdrawing his hand from hers, he lowered it to the cushion beside his hip, mirroring the placement of his other hand. Doing so, pulled at his gaping collar and captured her avid gaze.

"Je me rends." I surrender.

Her grandfather had always told her, when an enemy surrenders, do not hesitate, do not allow them the chance to contemplate their decision, do not falter in doing what had to be done. Of course, Adrien was not her enemy and this was not a field of battle, but the lesson could still be applied. She wasted no time in taking advantage of his acquiesce.

The top half of his shirt parted under her touch. She pulled the linen wide, exposing his right nipple, the dark, coppery disc surrounding it, and a smattering of hairs that matched the tawny shade of his brows. She laid her finger over his nipple without thinking. His breath hitched, forcing her gaze to his face. He had his eyes closed and his head thrown all the way back. The chords of his neck called to her in a way she feared might be more feral than domestic. But it was a siren call she was too weak to resist.

Leaning forward, she pressed her lips to the side of his neck. His flesh was hot against her mouth, his pulse rapid. She flicked out her tongue, causing him to swallow. The action bobbed his Adam's apple against her cheek. It was a most singular sensation. Another flick of her tongue prompted the same response, but when she ran her tongue up his neck toward his jaw, his reaction was much different. Burying a hand in the back of her hair, he pulled her away from his neck.

Gasping, Eirene stared down at Adrien's eyes, open and dark as a storm cloud.

"Was that unpleasant?" Simply because she enjoyed the feel of his mouth upon her neck did not guarantee he had enjoyed hers upon his.

He shook his head, then used the grip in her hair to force her mouth down upon his. The kiss curled her toes with its ferocity. He attacked with all weapons firing. Lips angled to force hers wide for the hard thrust of his tongue, teeth nipping at her bottom lip as he withdrew before unleashing another assault. When he sucked her full upper lip into his mouth, she melted into his embrace with a shuddering moan.

"You taste like heaven and smell like home." He spoke against her mouth, getting the words out in between drags upon her upper lip. "Holding you, kissing you, is like lying in a warm field of wildflowers."

Eirene pushed against his chest in order to end the kiss. She licked the taste of him from her lips while staring into his steady gaze. "With such honeyed words, it is no wonder ladies fall at your feet each season."

He sat up, forcing their bodies closer and their eyes level. "I have never spoken those words to another."

His intensity frightened her. No. She was not being honest. Her reaction to his intensity frightened her. His words did strange things to her insides. Her heart stuttered. Her lungs began to burn. Were her eyes watering?

Eirene blinked away the moisture. "This is not going the way I had planned."

"I did warn you it might not."

"I can be a bit stubborn."

He laughed at that, the response shaking his body and, in turn, hers. Yet another singular sensation she was not likely to forget any time soon.

"What are we to do now?" Her voice shook around the question.

"We should stop."

"Stop? Why?" There was no need to have oodles of experience to know he was aroused. His pulse raced as quickly as hers. His skin felt just as hot. She imagined her eyes shone just as bright as well. She had tasted his arousal in his kiss. She could *feel* it pressed between her thighs.

"We should stop because I do not want to."

After a moment of trying to sort the riddle, she shook her head. "I'm not certain I understand."

"I want to make love to you, Eirene. I want it like I have never wanted anything else in my entire life, except maybe for the return of my parents, but I do not want it like this." He shifted his gaze toward the small room at her back. "You deserve more than this as your first experience."

"I am not a virgin fresh from the school room, Adrien."

His gaze found hers once more. "No, but you are a virgin. You deserve better than a quick tup on a bloody uncomfortable settee. Hell, *I* want more than a quick tup on a bloody uncomfortable settee. I want you in my bed."

Eirene had to look away from Adrien's expression. There was too much there for her to comprehend. Focusing on the hand she had spread against his chest, she shook her head. "It is not part of the plan to share your bed."

"To hell with your damn plan, Eirene." He flexed his grip upon her hair to get her to look at him. "Do you truly think what is going on between us right now has anything to do with your scheme? Does what you're feeling feel like a damn business arrangement?"

She considered lying, but it was not within her power to hurt him, and she knew that particular falsehood would cause pain.

"No, it does not." Her honesty surprised him, and he made no attempt to hide the fact. "You expected me to deny it?"

"Oui."

"My grandfather always told me it is the mark of strength to know when to admit you were wrong. I was wrong about all of this." She tried to slide from his lap, but he loosed his grip from her hair and took hold of her waist with both hands, keeping her precisely where she was. "I should have chosen a different candidate. Westhaven, perhaps."

"Had you done that, I would have had to challenge Westhaven to a duel, and I've no wish to risk killing a friend."

She smiled at the jest. At least she hoped he spoke in jest. "This is a disaster."

Before Adrien could respond, a voice sounded from just outside the door. "For heaven's sake, why the devil would my presence be required in a servant's closet? I have a house full of guests. I cannot be expected to satisfy your every whim, Lucille. No wonder your husband—"

"Do shut up and open the door, Mary."

The door opened. "Saints alive!" Lady Palmer's shriek was a tad shy of glass shattering. She stood frozen in the doorway, staring at Eirene and Adrien, who stared back at her.

Adrien broke the awkward silence first. "This is not what it looks like, my lady."

His voice seemed to snap Lady Palmer out of her trance. "I daresay it is precisely what it looks like, *Monsieur Vicomte*."

Her words were shrill and loud. *Very* loud. And they effectively called the flock to their leader. In seconds, or so it seemed, the corridor behind Lady Palmer's quivering headpiece filled with the *crème de la crème* of London Society. They peered over her shoulder with wide eyes and feigned horror, all the while snickering behind their fans and eating up the sight of Adrien's bared chest.

It took every ounce of Eirene's self-possession to recall this was precisely what she had planned to have happen. In fact, present circumstances exceeded her expectations for she had not imagined the lady of the house as key witness. No one would question Lady Palmer's account of the incident. They would not dare.

Lady Palmer's focus zeroed in upon Eirene. "I must say, my lady, I am shocked. *Beyond* shocked, truth be told, that you would come into *my* house only to engage in…" She fluttered a gloved, bejeweled hand toward Adrien. "*This*."

"The lady is not to blame." Adrien managed a quick glance toward Eirene before lifting her from his lap so he could stand. A collective sigh issued forth from their audience as he did so. With his waistcoat open and his shirt undone but still tucked in, there was nothing to hide the evidence of his arousal as it strained the confines of his tight breeches.

To make matters worse, he spread his arms. "As you can see, ladies, nothing untoward has occurred."

Eirene gaped at Adrien. What was he doing? Aside from drawing attention to his…well, his… She glanced where all the other women were glancing. Why was he claiming nothing happened? That was most certainly *not* part of the plan.

Lady Palmer let out a noise of abject disbelief. "My *lord*, we can all see *quite* clearly what was within moments of transpiring." Her gaze flicked to Eirene, taking in the undone bodice and the excess of flesh above her stays. "I do hope you intend to accept this man's proposal of marriage, my lady."

Eirene opened her mouth, but it was Adrien who spoke. "I've no intention to propose." He glanced her way and winked. Ah. Smart man.

"No intention of proposing?" Lady Palmer's shriek sounded like a bad note on an out of tune violin. "You will most certainly propose to Lady Rowe-Weston, young man."

"I think not. "As calm as you please, Adrien began putting his clothes to rights. They all stared as he fashioned his cravat into an impressive knot without the aid of a mirror. When he was back in order, he turned to Eirene and bowed. "It has been my pleasure, my lady, though I do wish we had not been interrupted before I could enjoy more than just the fine taste of your lips."

Gasps, twitters, and a few sighs resulted from his shocking words.

Eirene had no idea how to react. This was the plan. Well, maybe not *The* Plan, but he seemed intent upon upholding his end of the bargain despite the change in tactic. A wise woman, which she prided herself upon being, would cease gaping and play her part as well.

She snapped her mouth closed and lifted her chin to stare down her nose. "You are a cad of the first order, Vicomte Benoit, to leave a lady unsatisfied after such boastful promises."

More gasps from the doorway.

He bowed. "You need only name the time and place, and I will do my best to rectify your disappointment."

"Well!" Lady Palmer stalked farther into the room and halted before Adrien. Her headdress quivered with rage as she lifted a gloved hand and smacked him soundly across the face.

Eirene pressed her hand to her mouth to stifle a gasp.

Adrien clenched his jaw, then cocked his head to the left then right, as if working out any discomfort caused by Lady Palmer's slap. "You possess a formidable strength, my lady."

Lady Palmer continued to quiver. "You will vacate my house this instant, you no good cad. As for you, my *lady*"—she turned her ire upon Eirene—"consider my son off limits."

With that, she gathered her skirts, tossed her head, and left the room. The other women, although seemingly reluctant to do so, followed in her wake.

"Her son?"

Eirene ignored Adrien's question and collapsed onto the settee. "That was awful." Her hands shook as she tried to retie her bodice ribbon.

"Here, allow me." Adrien crouched in front of her and shooed her hands away so that he might see to the task himself. With impressive efficiency, he executed the perfect little bow. "Are you all right?"

She forced herself to look him in the eye. "I imagine, after all that, I am officially ruined."

"So it would appear." He pushed to his feet, then paced away from her. The smallness of the room did not allow for much distance. Reaching the desk, he turned and leaned against it. "What happens now, Eirene?"

"I suppose we should leave, as Lady Palmer—"

"With us. What happens now, for us? Am I to bow over your hand, thank you for an entertaining evening, then see myself to hell?"

She flinched. "Of course not." She rubbed her damp palms along her skirt. "Why would you even suggest such a thing?"

"Because if you tell me our arrangement has been successfully concluded, or that my presence in your life is no longer required, or some other cold, calculating farewell, hell is precisely where you will send me."

She should have scolded him for being dramatic, but the words died in her throat. Legs trembling, heart racing, she stood. "We should be grateful Lady Palmer arrived when she did." Though Adrien did not seem inclined toward gratefulness at the moment. Clearing her throat, she tried again. "Had the situation progressed further, I imagine parting would prove more difficult."

"You admit to some difficulty in saying goodbye." It was not a question, more a surprised statement that she might actually possess human emotion. Not that she blamed him for the tone. After all, she lived her life in a very precise fashion, one that did not allow for an onslaught of *feeling*.

"Of course I find this difficult, *monsieur*."

"A few moments ago, I was Adrien." He left the desk and closed the distance between them, but he did not touch her. She thanked the heavens for that small favor. "I do not wish for this to be the end, Eirene."

"You speak of wishing to have me in your bed." Strange how easy it was to speak such bold words on the heels of their intimacy.

He touched her then. Taking hold of her shoulders in his strong, sure hands and applying just enough pressure to ensure she paid close attention to his next words. "That is not all I want."

"Adrien, do not." She lifted a hand and pressed her fingers to his lips. "I beg you to say no more. I submit that this was likely a horrible idea, but it is done, and I believe it has accomplished what I intended. Whatever might have stirred to life between us in this room must be laid to rest." Did her words sound as hollow as she felt saying them?

She lowered her hand. "I want you to be assured, the information you shared about your past will never cross my lips. Consider that your pay—"

With a heated curse, he released her and stalked from the room.

Eirene, left shaken and confused by Adrien's abrupt departure, stood staring at the open door until a servant, sent by Lady Palmer, asked if she required assistance in locating the exit.

****

"Dare I inquire as to how your evening went?"

Adrien, who stood with his forehead pressed against the cool panes of his bedroom window, did not so much as move a muscle at Cyril's arrival. "I believe

122

I played my part to Lady Rowe-Weston's satisfaction." The words fogged up the glass, but he hadn't been admiring the view, so it did not matter.

"Must I wait to read the details in tomorrow's paper?"

"Do you believe a person can fall in love after only a brief acquaintance, *mon ami*?" Silence filled the space at Adrien's back, a silence so deep and so alarming, he turned to make sure Cyril had not fainted or expired. His friend stood in the center of the room, dressed in his favorite, flowing, emerald green banyan and house slippers, staring at Adrien as though he had sprouted a tail.

"Love?" Cyril managed to croak. "You fancy yourself in *love* with Lady Rowe-Weston?" He shook his head while raking a hand through his soft, pomade free curls. "Was she *that* good?" Cyril threw up his hands as Adrien moved away from the window. "Forgive me. That was in poor taste. But love? Are you certain you do not simply fancy this woman?"

"I fancied the butcher's daughter when I was thirteen." Adrien looked out over the moonlit garden again. "This does not feel like that." The aforementioned fascination had lasted the duration of one summer. The object of said fascination had been five years older than he, quick to smile, quicker to flirt, and more than willing to buss a thirteen-year-old lad on the lips a time or two. He had been infatuated with that eighteen year old vixen, and now he could not even recall the color of her hair or her name. No, this did not feel like that.

He had no doubt that in twenty years, if anyone were to ask, he would be able to tell them Eirene possessed dark auburn hair, bright copper eyes, and exactly forty-three freckles on her left cheek. He would also recall the way she smelled. That wildflower fragrance of hers would likely haunt him in his grave. As would the slight weight of her shifting upon his lap. The sight of her breasts straining to be free of her stays. Her taste.

And worst of all. Most tormenting of all. He would never forget the look on her face as she promised to keep his truth a secret as *payment*.

"Did you confess your feelings to the lady?"

"Not in so many words." When Adrien turned from the window, it was to find Cyril seated upon the bed with his voluminous banyan gathered around him and his slippered feet dangling a few inches above the floor. "I do not believe she would have taken kindly to such a confession. The lady is quite determined to spend the rest of her days rusticating in solitude out in the country."

"Really, Adrien, I am shocked to have to state what should be obvious."

"And that is?"

"Tell her how you feel."

Adrien shook his head. "She will not have me."

Cyril hopped off the bed and swept toward Adrien. "For heaven's sake, you daft fool. If the lost, pathetic, forlorn expression upon your face is that of love, then do whatever you must to change her mind."

Chapter Ten

Eirene allowed herself to sleep in the next morning. Usually, she was up at dawn, despite the rest of the city's preference to laze about in bed until noon. But not today. Sleep had eluded her last night, and the mere thought of crawling out of bed made her want to cry and carry on like a petulant child. She blamed Adrien. He had taken hold of her emotions, her sanity, and her ability to reason and thrown all of it into a stinking pile of refuse. Then he had stomped upon it for good measure with his talk of wanting *more*.

Damn the man to hell for his inability to act like an unscrupulous rogue.

She had been unable to form a single thought that did not involve the vexing man, and even worse, she had relived every moment of their rendezvous over and over again until her body burned with unsatisfied arousal. She hoped he had spent an equally insufferable night. It was the least he deserved after leaving her stranded and alone to face Lady Palmer's renewed wrath.

The woman had confronted Eirene as she had attempted to leave unnoticed. Again, Lady Palmer had reiterated that her son and his ten thousand a year were off limits. She'd not align her family with a fallen woman. Eirene had said nothing, though she had longed to tell Lady Palmer exactly what she could do with her son's ten thousand a year and her illogical assumption Eirene would ever wish to have anything to do with the man.

Her bedroom door opened, and Hamish peeked his head in. Upon seeing her awake, he entered bearing a tray consisting of a pot of tea, her favorite cup, the morning paper, and what looked to be a pile of correspondence.

"I would wish you good morning, my lady, but seeing as how it is half noon…" He allowed the censure in his tone to state the rest. Setting the tray atop her vanity, he poured a cup of steaming, fragrant tea and carried it and the paper to the bed.

Eirene sat up against the pillows and accepted the cup with both hands. After a few sips, she reached for the paper. Hamish had folded it open to reveal the Society page. She glanced up at her hovering butler. "Do you now work for a social pariah, Hamish?"

"It would seem so, my lady." With a bow, he left her to read the accounting of her night.

Dearest readers,

Where do I begin?

Lady P's annual ball will go down in history. This author has it on good authority, not to mention personal observation, that a certain Lady of Great Wealth was caught in the throes of a passionate embrace with a certain dashing Frenchman. The couple was discovered by none other than Lady P herself and, when confronted, acted in the most shocking way imaginable.

Our dashing Frenchman, displaying masculine attributes that surely belong in a museum, claimed nothing untoward had occurred. He went so far as to confess to the Lady of Great Wealth it was his wish to find an opportunity in the future to enjoy more than just her kiss.

Can you imagine?

When pressed by Lady P to make an honest woman of the wealthy lady, he refused! *I tremble at the audacity of such a response. And yet, that, my dearest readers, was not* the most shocking *turn of events. Oh no, for the Lady of Great Wealth labeled our Dashing Frenchman a* cad *for leaving her* unsatisfied! *Faced with such outrageous behavior, Lady P did what any of us would have done. She ordered the shocking creatures to vacate her home with all haste, adding that her son was now off limits to the likes of Lady R-W.*

This author must confess no prior knowledge of an understanding between Lady P's son and Lady R-W and imagines such a match existed only in Lady P's mind.

Eirene folded the paper and set it aside without finishing the article. She had read enough to conclude The Plan had been a success. She was a fallen woman. Ruined. An outcast. Returning to the country would be expected of her. By next Season, she would be forgotten, replaced by a bevy of debutantes and wealthy widows.

A smile curled her lips as she sipped her tea. Should she send Adrien a note of gratitude? After all, his performance had been worthy of an ovation. Before and after Lady Palmer entered the room.

Blast! She refused to spend another moment dwelling on the moments prior to Lady Palmer's appearance. She had packing to do and a quiet country life awaiting her return. Allowing the relief to build into a feeling of euphoria, she absentmindedly reached for the pile of correspondence that Hamish had laid upon the bed. There were at least fifty cards. She picked up the first.

It took her a moment to register what she was seeing, but when she did, she threw the card as if it had turned into a large, furry spider.

Hand shaking, she shuffled through the rest, most containing names of gentlemen who had plagued her since her arrival in London. This should not be happening. Had none of them seen the morning paper? Did they not realize she was ruined? The last thing any of them should seek was a moment of her time. A scrawled note on the back of Lord Crestwald's card caught her attention. The man claimed to have been captivated by her beauty upon seeing her at Lady Palmer's ball. He went on to express a willingness to overlook her moment of misguided judgment.

Moment of misguided judgment? Was the man mad? She'd been caught sitting astride a rake's lap, for pity's sake. Another moment and it was likely she would have been *impaled* by said rake. And Lord Crestwald was willing to overlook it because she was beautiful? It seemed he was not alone. Card after card claimed much the same, a willingness to forgive, forget, and *protect*.

Realization dawned as she stared at the choice of words written on the back of Lord Bristow's card. He offered his protection. He owned a lovely cottage in the Lake District. She would have *carte blanche*.

Good God! These men did not wish to marry her. They wished to set her up as their mistress. It seemed her rendezvous with Adrien had only managed to replace one dilemma with another. Twenty-four hours ago, these men coveted her money. Now they coveted *her*.

What the devil was she to do now?

Dropping the cards, she grabbed her wrap and hurried from her bedroom. Tying the belt as she walked, she headed for her study. She always thought best within the confines of her study. A fire blazed in the hearth, and she sent a silent blessing for the existence of Hamish. Locating a sheet of blank paper, she quickly folded it in half, then flattened it atop the blotter. She did not bother to sit down. Hunched over, unbound hair dangling precariously close to the ink, she dipped her pen and began to outline the pros and cons of a new plan.

A little over an hour later, both sides of the paper were full, neither one boasting more support than the other.

"Blast!" Why was it that, ever since she had come to London, she had not been able to make a definitive decision one way or the other? Setting aside the list, she opened the top drawer and grabbed a single shilling from the stash of random coins. She flipped it into the air, caught it deftly, then slapped it upside down on the top of her other hand. Before uncovering the coin, she decided tails would mean going forth with the new plan.

She took a deep breath and revealed the coin. Tails.

Well, there it was. One could not argue with physics, or so her grandfather always said. Putting the coin back in the desk, she headed to her bedroom to change. She had not a moment to lose, not if she still wished to be sleeping in the country come evening.

A little over an hour later, Eirene stood in Cyril

Petley's foyer suffering the disapproving opinion of the man's butler. "This is highly improper, my lady."

The servant glanced over Eirene's shoulder to the world beyond the still-open, front door. With agitated movements, he reached past her to close the door then turned, holding her card as if it might combust.

"*Highly* improper," he repeated, with emphasis.

"Yes, thank you for your unsolicited concern for my reputation." Removing her bonnet and pelisse, she thrust both at the butler, forcing him to either do his duty or allow the articles to fall to the floor. Thankfully, for the sake of her favorite pelisse, he did his duty. "Now then, is Vicomte Benoit home to callers?"

"Lady Rowe-Weston, I presume?"

Eirene turned to address the query. It came from a man in the process of descending the stairs. Though she did not know him, she assumed he was none other than Cyril Petley. An assumption he confirmed by dismissing the butler with naught but a nod before reaching her and accepting the hand she extended.

"Cyril Petley, at your service, my lady." He blew a kiss above her knuckles, then straightened with a smile that possessed the power to shine right through his light brown eyes. It was a sight genuine enough to counter the roundness of his features and the girth straining the buttons of his waistcoat. Mister Petley would never make young ladies swoon upon first glance, but if given the chance, he would make their hearts sing.

"I do apologize for invading your home in such an improper fashion, Mister Petley." Eirene glanced up the staircase, wondering if Adrien was within earshot.

"No need to apologize."

"I believe your butler would say otherwise." They

shared a smile, but the moment was short lived as Eirene recalled the urgency behind her visit. "I've come to see Adrien."

The name rolled off her tongue as though a part of her vernacular for decades.

Petley, to his credit, did not flinch at the informality. "Might I ask why?"

Had the man suddenly stripped off his clothing and asked her to dance a reel, she could not have been more shocked. While debating whether to respond to the rather invasive question, Petley revealed his true colors. That of a protective ally.

"Permit me to say, my lady, Adrien passed a rather unsettled night." The statement was instantly recognizable for what it was intended to be, a placement of blame. "I cannot begin to guess whether he will wish to see you or not."

"I see." Eirene attempted to ignore the heat that climbed from her neck to her cheeks. She should have chosen a lighter gown, it seemed, one with not so high a collar. "Might I presume upon your hospitality by asking you to inquire directly?"

She could not help but wonder what Petley knew of her rendezvous with Adrien. Something had clearly awoken the guard dog within the man. Something Adrien had said? Or was it simply a case of Petley having decided not to like her? The latter seemed likely. She was well aware of her ability to be off-putting. Hadn't Adrien, himself, said as much when commending her foresight to avoid marriage?

"Before I decide whether or not to encourage a meeting, will you indulge me by answering a simple question?"

"If I am able, certainly." She fisted her hands at her sides to avoid rubbing them together in anxious impatience. She was not accustomed to being challenged, and Mister Petley, despite kind looks and smiling eyes, proved a formidable challenger.

"What are your intentions toward Adrien, my lady?"

"My intentions?" What the devil? Petley spoke as though Adrien's reputation teetered on the brink. How ridiculous. Despite the events of the previous evening, the article in the paper had managed to be rather flattering where Adrien was concerned. He'd not lack female attention when next he ventured into Society, of that she was certain. And if he ever wished to marry, no doubt there would be a long line of willing brides.

The tea she had consumed that morning soured in her stomach. Though why the thought of Adrien walking down the aisle would cause her insides to rebel, she hadn't a clue. What the man did with his future had nothing to do with her. Well, not beyond the next twenty-four hours, at least.

But first she had to actually *see* Adrien and lay out her new plan.

"My lady?"

Eirene snapped to attention, determined to have done with Petley's impromptu interrogation. "You need not worry about the welfare of your friend, Mister Petley. I simply require a brief moment of Adrien's time in order to make a slight adjustment to our arrangement."

"I was under the impression said arrangement ended with this morning's gossip."

"Yes, well, there has been a slight setback." She

prayed he would not press for details. It would be rather embarrassing to admit to the number of men wishing to set her up in a nice cottage in lieu of luring her down the aisle. Odd for them to suddenly covet her body more than her wealth. Such nonsense only occurred when a woman possessed ethereal beauty, and she knew she did not, never mind the silly declarations to the contrary that had been scribbled upon the calling cards. Since when were freckles *fetching*? No, it was all ludicrous and in need of a quick resolution.

Petley hooked his thumbs into the waist of his trousers and shifted his impressive weight from one foot to the other. "A setback, you say? My curiosity is almost painful, my lady." He held up a hand to silence her before she could speak. "No, no, I'll respect your right to privacy, but do allow me to offer you a small warning, hmm?"

"Of course." A shiver of foreboding chased away the heat that had suffused her face.

"Do not hurt him, my lady. He has suffered enough in this lifetime."

It took a moment for Eirene to find her voice. "I've no desire to make him suffer."

Petley held her gaze with a searching look. "Sometimes we are not permitted to choose the end result of our actions, my lady." On that rather cryptic note, he informed her Adrien had yet to emerge from his rooms but had rung for coffee and the valet. "You should find him awake and decent, my lady." After offering directions to Adrien's private chambers, he bowed and bid her a pleasant, good day.

Eirene shivered in the wake of Petley's departure. She had to admire the man for wishing to protect his friend. It spoke well of his character, but the words he had chosen continued to echo in her mind. *He has suffered enough in this lifetime.* Had some of that suffering been at her hands? Adrien had been angry upon leaving her last night, but had the anger been fueled by pain? Had her rejection hurt him? Had he returned home and confessed as much to Petley?

It seemed incredibly unlikely that she possessed the power to hurt a man of Adrien's confidence. Did he even like her? Yes, he claimed to want her, but he had never said he *liked* her. One could not be emotionally hurt by someone they did not care for. In fact, the deeper the affection, the greater the pain. It was obvious Petley assumed there was something more between herself and Adrien, but he was wrong. Their arrangement did not allow for inconvenient emotions, and it certainly did not require an attachment or deep affections.

No, despite Petley's concern, Adrien's heart was safe from harm while in her company. Once they parted ways, it would be intact if he wished to offer it to some unknown recipient in the—

Blast! She pressed a hand to her rolling stomach. She would have to ask Hamish if he had accidentally brought her spoiled tea at breakfast.

Back to the matter at hand. As for her own heart, that bothersome organ had not stirred to life since she'd watched her grandfather's coffin being entombed. It would take a great deal more than practiced kisses, warm hands, and honeyed words to awaken it after all these years.

"Why am I even thinking about hearts, awakened or otherwise," she mumbled as she gathered her skirts and mounted the stairs. By this time tomorrow, she'd be settled back in the country, London and all of its distractions firmly behind her.

That included a particular Frenchman in possession of practiced kisses, warm hands, honeyed words, and a tantalizing collarbone.

"Do get a handle on your musings, Eirene. For pity's sake, you've the mind of a woman trapped in a lurid novel."

"My lady?"

Eirene halted halfway up the stairs and turned to find Petley's butler hovering at the bottom, look of disapproval firmly in place. "Yes?"

Of course he had likely overheard her conversation with herself, but she'd not mention it and no servant worth their salary would either.

"Pardon my boldness, my lady, but you're going the wrong direction if you mean to leave." He jerked a thumb over his shoulder. "The street lies beyond the same door you entered."

Grinding her teeth in an effort not to scold the man for his impertinence, Eirene somehow managed a smile, albeit one that likely looked a tad disingenuous. "I am not attempting to locate the exit, but thank you for your service. I shall leave a good word about you to your master before I depart."

She turned her back on the gaping butler and continued up the stairs, careful to keep her thoughts to herself lest she give the man something further to discuss below stairs with his fellow servants.

After all, appearing without a chaperone upon the front stoop of a bachelor's home was quite enough fodder to keep the servants gasping and tittering over their midday meal.

****

Adrien lay abed, staring at the canopy. The maid had come and gone with his coffee, which sat, untouched and cold, on a table across the room. The valet had made three attempts to coerce him to rise and dress, going so far as to lay a set of clothes across the foot of the bed, but Adrien lacked the motivation to stir. He'd gotten little to no sleep, thanks to a certain freckled vixen who had no desire to clap eyes on him ever ag—

"My God! I was told you were awake and decent."

Adrien shot upright as Eirene's voice pierced the silence of his vast bedchamber. She stood in the doorway, one hand over her mouth, the other pressed to her stomach. She looked beautiful, dressed in a dark green walking dress with a subtle edging of black lace about the hem and high collar. Her hair, unbound and glorious, caught the sunlight that spilled into his room from between the curtains the maid had pulled open without permission.

He made a mental note to kiss the maid when next he encountered her. On the cheek, of course. He had no desire to kiss any lips that were not located upon the face of the woman presently glowering at him as if he had lured her into a den of sin.

"What are you doing in my room, Eirene?" Belatedly, and thanks to the direction of Eirene's wide gaze, he recalled his habit of sleeping in the nude. He glanced down to find the sheet safely pooled in his lap. For good measure, he tugged it a little higher lest his body decide to acknowledge her sudden appearance in a very inappropriate manner.

"I've come to discuss an amendment to our arrangement, but clearly this is not—"

"I was under the impression our arrangement ended last night?" He hadn't seen the morning paper. Hadn't wished to. No doubt it contained a sumptuous report of their behavior at Lady Palmer's ball with details aplenty to see Eirene thoroughly ruined and his reputation as a rake unthreatened.

"Yes, had things progressed as planned, you would be correct." While speaking, she walked farther into the room and closed the door. He did not fail to notice the way she kept her gaze averted from the bed, and it made him want to lunge to his feet, *sans* sheet, and beg her to pet every inch of his body. It was the very fantasy that had kept him awake all night, the thought of her hands moving over his flesh, followed by the fullness of her lips and perhaps the moisture of her tongue.

Jesu! The sheet stirred over his hardening cock, and he slapped a hand over his lap.

Meanwhile, unaware of his growing agony, Eirene wandered toward the fireplace. She halted beside the untouched breakfast tray and picked up the unread newspaper. "Have you seen the gossip?" She threw the question over her shoulder without looking at him.

"I have not."

"It was quite accurate and damning." She laid the paper back down, then fondled the lid of the coffee pot. He wished she would not. "Needless to say, I was elated upon reading it, believing my reputation to be in tatters."

Adrien frowned at her choice of words. "Eirene? What has occurred?"

Abandoning the coffee pot, she drifted the rest of the distance to the fireplace. Her hand trailed along the edge of the mantle, hesitating as her fingers drew even with a small, framed portrait. She leaned close, and he braced for the inevitable question.

"What a lovely portrait."

"Oui." The image was of himself, Cyril, and Sir and Lady Petley. It had been commissioned months prior to his seventeenth birthday, or as he believed at the time, to commemorate Adrien Benoit's seventeenth birthday and two year anniversary of life among the Petley's. The artist had done an excellent job capturing the warmth that had existed within the small family. A warmth that had included him from the very beginning but one he had never known to be authentic.

Maybe someday he would allow the betrayal to fade away like a bad memory, but for now, it still rankled.

"How old were you?"

"Not quite seventeen."

She surprised him by sending a direct smile over her shoulder. "And already breaking hearts, I imagine?"

"Not to my knowledge."

"You are too modest." Her smile faltered, and she turned away once more. "I received numerous calling cards from various gentlemen this morning, Adrien."

He sat up a little straighter, his instincts going on full alert at her use of his name, coupled with the slight roughening of her voice.

"At first, I believed the gentlemen were renewing their efforts to win my hand despite my scandalous behavior."

"They were not?" *Mon Dieu,* if the calling cards

were what he suspected—

"They were offering *carte blanche*."

To hell with propriety. Adrien left the bed and went to Eirene. She visibly stiffened but made no move to avoid his touch as he took hold of her shoulders and gently spun her to face him. "I demand to know their names."

Her smile was as brittle as old paint. "You cannot think to challenge *all* of them."

"I can and I will."

"No, you will not." She slipped free of his grasp and brushed by him, close enough to drag her hem along the tops of his bare feet. He shivered at the contact. "I have formulated a new plan to counter this unwanted development." She glanced back, then quickly away. "I will need your help."

Adrien returned to the bed to tug the sheet free and wrap it about his hips. "You can turn around, Eirene." She gave a little peek first, then turned to face him, her gaze drifting along his exposed torso then up his neck to finally find his eyes. *Jesu*, her look could boil water. He forced himself to focus on the matter at hand. "What do you need me to do?"

She twisted her hands together, then buried them in the folds of her skirt. "It is obvious I have successfully rendered myself unmarriageable, but now I am tasked with having to render myself unfit to be a mistress."

"Short of contracting some foul disease, I do not see how you could possibly—"

"You and I must become engaged."

It took Adrien a moment to shake free of his thoughts and process what she had said. "Engaged?" He croaked the word as if a frog had lodged itself in his throat. "I thought the entire point of this maddening endeavor of yours was to *avoid* marriage?"

"Becoming affianced does not have to mean marriage, Adrien."

"In *my* world it most certainly does."

"We are not discussing your world or even the real world. We are discussing my great dilemma and how best to solve the latest development."

"An engagement is not the solution. Trust me." Was the woman daft? Could she not see the complications that would surely arise from such an—

"It is the only solution."

Adrien bit the inside of his cheek and counted to ten so as not to give into the urge to grab her by the shoulders and shake some sense into her. When he felt in control of his emotions, he attempted to explain why her view of things was askew. "Couples who are affianced have a tendency to anticipate their vows."

"I see." She shifted her focus away from him while worrying her lower lip with her teeth. A deep look of contemplation came over her followed by a brightening of her copper eyes that should have served as a warning, and yet, Adrien was still caught unaware when she said, "Anticipating the vows is an excellent idea."

Lord have mercy on his soul. The woman was a loon. A beautiful, sweet-smelling, deliciously curved loon.

He raked a hand through his sleep tangled hair. "It is a terrible idea." God help him if she asked him to expl—

"Nonsense. If we become engaged, then call off the arrangement after we have anticipated our vows, surely the scandal will be extraordinary? No man wants a notorious mistress, do they?" She clapped her hands together. "It is brilliant!"

He backed up for fear she meant to hug him in triumph. "It is not brilliant. It is yet another one of your schemes doomed to fail because you have not considered the consequences."

"I am quite certain your reputation will survive a broken engagement, Adrien."

"That is not the consequence I speak of." He moved closer, forcing her to back up until she bumped the edge of a chair.

She put up her hands but did not place them against his bare chest. "Must you stand so close?"

"Oui." Proximity would help him make his point.

She lowered her hands, oh so carefully so as not to brush even a single fingertip against his skin. The caution made him want to grab her hands and put them all over his body, beginning with the parts under the sheet.

"What consequence do you speak of then?" Her voice had lowered an octave, and he could not mistake the sudden fluttering of her pulse at the base of her throat for anything other than what it was. Arousal.

He fixed his attention upon that pulse point long enough to make her breath catch, then he slowly dragged his gaze up until it clashed with hers. "You have not considered the consequence of allowing me inside your body."

Her eyes flared wide, her mouth fell open, and a wash of bright red suffused her freckled cheeks. "Well, I…I mean to say…"

She took another step back, but there was nowhere to go but into the chair. The sudden shift in elevation put her eye level with his groin. A gentleman would have stepped back. He certainly would not have leaned forward and braced his hands upon the chair arms.

He felt the sheet part over his left thigh. If he weren't careful, the damn thing would fall off into Eirene's lap. Funny, at the moment he could not fathom why that would be bad.

"Given your reputation as a rake, I highly doubt the two of us—" She gestured wildly. "—would leave that lasting of an impression upon you."

"And what of you?" He bent his arms to bring his face closer. "What if being intimate leaves a lasting impression upon yourself? Have you thought of that?"

She turned her face away. "I am far too sensible to allow such an act to—"

"Eirene."

She snapped her mouth shut and turned to face him. "Is this the part where you kiss me in an attempt to prove a point?" Despite the scolding tone, her gaze drifted toward his mouth.

He smiled. "No." That earned him a narrow glare. "This is the part when I tell you to touch me."

"Touch you?" She nearly shrieked the question.

"Go on. Anywhere you wish."

She frantically shook her head. "That is a horrible idea."

"Why?" *Go on, admit it.* "Are you afraid?"

Her chin came up as she drew her shoulders back. "Afraid? Of what? Touching you? Ha! It is not as though doing so will injure me. I touched you last night, and here I sit, hale and hearty."

"Then go ahead," he goaded. "I dare you."

Chapter Eleven

Goodness, he had dared her to touch him.

The last time anyone had dared Eirene to do anything, she had ended up flat on her back, unable to breathe for several moments. Touching Adrien would hardly end the same as her failed attempt to climb a stupid tree. First of all, she was sitting down. One could not fall and end up flat on their back from such a position. Secondly, if she did not fall, there was no threat of knocking the air from her lungs so breathing should not be an issue.

All in all, there seemed no logical reason to ignore the dare.

Besides, as she had pointed out to him, she had already touched him. She had touched his collarbone. His chest. His lips. Why did he believe the current situation different? Her gaze skittered across his very bare chest. Unlike last night's touching, which had been conducted while he had remained fully clothed, save for jacket and cravat, he stood before her now in naught but a sheet. And a poorly knotted one at that. If he so much as sneezed…

"I am waiting."

Decision made, she reached out and traced the ridge of his collarbone. It felt much the same as it had the previous night. Reaching the end of the bone, she retraced her path back toward his throat then lowered her hand onto her lap and lifted her gaze to his.

"There. I touched you and am none the worse for wear for—"

He took hold of her hand and pressed it against the makeshift knot holding the sheet around his hips. "You touched me there last night so it does not satisfy the dare."

"You did not specify where I was—"

"Do not play coy, Eirene. It does not suit you."

"My grandfather would have agreed with you."

"Let us not bring your grandfather into this right now, hmm? I am not sure he would approve of where your hand is."

His words drew her attention to her hand. When the devil had she moved it from the knot at his hip to the top of his thigh? A little to the right and she would find herself with a handful of—

"Go on."

She imagined those two words, spoken precisely in that husky, seductive tone, had preceded Eve taking the apple from Satan. Adrien laughed when she said as much out loud.

"*Oui*, you likened me to the serpent and the apple upon on our first meeting, if you recall, but I am not Satan and it's not an apple I offer."

Careful not to move her hand even the slightest bit, she looked in his eyes. "Remind me what you are attempting to prove?"

"I am attempting to illustrate my belief that you will not be able to forget a moment of intimacy between us, but damned if I remember why."

"Because I claimed myself too sensible to allow such a thing?"

"*Oui*, that was it." He flicked his gaze toward her hand. "Well? Will you admit I am correct and discard your new scheme or will you prove me wrong and convince me to go along with the faux engagement?"

"You will agree to my new plan if I accept your dare?"

"*Oui*, but only if you manage to remain unaffected, and given the way you reacted to my kisses last evening, I'd say your chance of success is slim."

"Your kisses scramble my mind."

"But touching me will not?" He nodded once. "I see. Very well. Have at it."

Eirene curled her fingers around the edge of the knot. The sheet was fashioned from the softest linen, its hem edged with a thick band of satin. The color, a rich, deep burgundy. A perfect match to the gown she'd worn at their first meeting. Had he taken note of such a detail?

The backs of her fingers brushed the hardness of his hipbone as she tugged at the knot. He inhaled, forcing the muscles of his lower stomach to constrict. The knot gave way, and the weight of the blanket did the rest, leaving her hand hovering over the taut skin of his furred thigh. She made a fist in the air, suddenly unsure if any of this was wise. Perhaps there was another solution to her new dilemma? Another option not considered. A convent, for instance.

"Eirene?"

She shook her head and closed her eyes against the sight of her pale fist hovering close to his tantalizing thigh. Good heavens, had she ever wished to lay her hand upon anything as desperately as his flesh? To feel the crisp hairs and the muscle. A pain seared her chest.

Heavens, was that longing? Desire? Arousal? Hunger for *him*?

"Eirene?" He repeated her name then his hands framed her face.

She opened her eyes to look at him. "You win."

He shook his head while dropping to his knees. "No. This is not a game. I had no right to even hint otherwise. Forgive me."

"If I say you are forgiven, will you kiss me?"

"Do you want me to kiss you, Eirene?"

"Oui." He smiled at that, as she had hoped he might.

He leaned in then kissed her…*cheek?*

Eirene frowned. "I meant upon the mouth."

In one motion, he stood and dragged the sheet back around his hips. "I need a moment." Without further explanation, he left her sitting in the chair, staring after him as he crossed the room and passed through a narrow, paneled door, which he closed behind him.

Well then!

She spent a few minutes simply sitting in the chair before it occurred to her to do something productive. If the kiss she had requested progressed in the direction she suspected it may, the current chill in the room might prove inconvenient. Thankfully, everything she required to make a decent fire was at hand. In no time, thanks to the many lessons at her grandfather's side, a lovely blaze roared in the hearth. She poked at it a few times with the wolf's head fire iron then replaced the tool alongside its matching mate.

"There are servants on Cyril's payroll who cannot fashion as impressive a fire." Adrien had returned without making a sound. He stood directly behind her, his voice in her ear, his breath in her hair.

"My grandfather taught me many useful things."

His hands came to rest upon her shoulders. "Such as?"

She stared at the fire, wondering if he still wore the sheet. "How to shoot, ride, hunt, skin an animal, diagnose certain illnesses, treat a gunshot wound, the proper way to flush out an enemy, how to avoid an ambush, when to say no to a challenge and when to stand firm. Just to name a few."

"You loved him."

Her eyes began to burn so she looked away from the fire. "Yes. Very much. He was good to me."

"And your parents? Were they good to you?"

Why must he ask such things now? Shouldn't they be kissing? What man would rather talk than kiss?

"Were they?"

Hoping to put an end to his invasiveness, she offered a curt, "no." She should have suspected it would not satisfy.

He spun her within his arms. His hair was wet and slicked back, as if he had splashed water on his face then raked his hands through his hair. Droplets dotted his bare shoulders, and she watched as one tracked down toward his nipple. Without thinking, she leaned forward and caught it with her tongue before it could reach its destination.

****

Adrien felt as though he'd suddenly leapt into the fire Eirene so expertly started. If she meant to distract him from asking questions about her family, swiping her tongue across the top of his nipple was a damn good strategy. When she pressed her lips to his flesh and

147

moaned softly, he nearly laughed out loud at the level of torment her actions caused.

He had suggested to Cyril that he might love this woman. How else explain the power she wielded while doing almost nothing? The mere swipe of a tongue had never rendered him senseless. Ever. Lustful, eager, and impatient, yes, but never senseless. If asked to name the current King, he would not have been able to, not while Eirene dragged her warm mouth across his chest in a series of light, airy, butterfly kisses.

She reached his other nipple, and instead of teasing the upper edge, she attacked directly, flicking her tongue across the sensitive tip then sucking in a sharp breath as it responded by puckering into a hard nub.

She was going to kill him. Slowly and with extreme pleasure.

"This is a very bad idea." Although proud of himself for managing to speak without revealing the way he shook inside, he hated himself for the words. Logic was a poor bedfellow to lust.

She drew back and looked up at him. "As I recall, you dared me to touch you."

"I said nothing about employing your tongue to do so." His tone read a bit harsh as evidenced by the slight widening of her eyes.

"I see." She wiggled free of his hands and stepped back to cross her arms and glare. He wondered if her grandfather had helped her perfect the disapproving expression. "Let me see if I correctly understand the way of things, hmm? You offer yourself to me in a rather blatant fashion, I might add."

She raked her eyes down his body. He had replaced the sheet with a pair of loose, linen trousers. They sat low on his hips, and her gaze lingered in the vicinity of the waistband.

He glanced down and noted the swath of hair just visible above the ivory fabric. Obviously, the sheet had been more modest.

"As I was saying…" She returned her gaze to his. "You stand there all—" She flapped her hand in the air and shook her head as if the word she sought simply did not exist. "—and yet I am to adhere to rules I am unaware exist?"

"What?" She had lost him. "Who mentioned rules?"

"You forbade me to use my tongue. That sounds like a rule."

The image of her using her tongue to its fullest advantage had him regretting the looseness of his trousers. They tented rather embarrassingly over the rising enthusiasm of his cock. Did she really need him to explain what would happen if she continued to lick him? Maybe if he just gestured to draw her attention down…but, no, he had to remember this was a woman reared on military tactics not fantasies of love and romance.

"I was not laying down the rules, Eirene, merely cautioning you—"

"Against what?" While voicing the question, she glanced down. Color washed into her face, darkening her freckles. Her lips parted around a silent exclamation. "Oh." Very quickly, she spun to face the fire. "I will allow you a moment of privacy to see to…to do whatever it is…you need to do."

"I need to hold you."

She peeked over her shoulder. "You are quite adept

at this."

"You've lost me again."

"At being a rake." She turned toward him. "You are quite adept at rendering yourself irresistible to women."

"Does that mean you find me irresistible?" He bit back his smile and allowed himself a moment to admire how she looked with the fire behind her. The glow of the flames created an orange halo around her loose hair.

"Notice, I am managing to resist."

Now he smiled. "Of course you are, but tell me, is it hard?"

God help him, but she flicked her gaze toward his groin, turning his last word into an unintended double entendre.

"It would appear so." Her lips twitched as if she were the one now fighting back a smile.

Adrien held out his hand. "Show a little mercy and come here."

She slipped her hand into his without hesitation and allowed him to coax her closer. "How is my proximity merciful?" She laughed as he tugged her the remaining distance, causing her to fall against his body.

"Because it allows me to do this." He kissed her smiling lips.

****

Eirene coiled her arms around Adrien's neck, her fingers playing among the wet tips of his hair. He deepened their kiss with the slightest adjustment to the angle of his mouth, and schooled now in the way of things, she was ready when his tongue glided alongside hers. He tasted of mint, and she suspected the reason behind his brief absence was so that he might freshen himself up for her.

Strangely, the thought provoked a warm flush of pleasure and a small sound of joy.

Adrien eased back. "Are you laughing at my kisses, *mademoiselle*?"

"You cleaned your teeth."

He stared down at her for a confused moment, then nodded. *"Oui."*

"How gallant and, dare I say, not very rake-like."

"Has it occurred to you yet, my dearest, I might not actually *be* the rake you accuse me of being?"

"It has, yes." It seemed indelicate to offer anything other than honesty while being held in his arms. "And allow me to admit, the realization is bothersome."

"Oh?"

Eirene nodded. "Yes. I do believe I could handle you better if you were a dastardly rake intent upon ravishing me senseless before leaving me to wallow in regret and self-pity."

"But?"

"*But* you are not intending to do that, are you?"

"Not in the least." He frowned. "Why do I suspect that disappoints you?"

"Disappoints, no. Frightens? Yes." Heavens, there was a point when too much honesty did a person no favors. She may have reached said point. Uncomfortable, she pried herself from his embrace and stepped back. "Have we reached an agreement then?"

"I take it that question is intended to preempt what could have been a pleasurable rendezvous?"

She could not help it. She flicked her gaze beyond his partially clad body, toward the rumpled bed. What would it be like to spend a few hours in that canopied monstrosity? Not sleeping, of course. Heat crept into her face at the image of herself lying entangled with Adrien's naked limbs. Were she to end up in his bed, he would not merely hold her. He might not be a rake, but he was a man, and men did not merely hold the women they took into their beds. Her mother had not taught her a great deal of useful knowledge, but she had managed to impart that bit of wisdom.

"Eirene?"

She yanked her gaze from the bed to look at Adrien. "Will you agree to pose as my betrothed?"

He crossed his bare arms over his bare chest, transforming a rather mundane posture into something quite extraordinary thanks to the lovely muscles of his upper arms and the captivating tendons that stretched along the curve of his shoulders.

It was beyond her not to stare.

"How long will this farce continue?"

"Hmm?" She moved her focus toward that damnable collarbone of his and her mouth watered at the remembered taste and texture.

"How long will we be engaged?"

"As long as it takes," she replied, rather absently, while allowing her gaze to travel up the side of his neck. There was a drop of water just below his ear. She licked her bottom lip so as not to step forward and lick his neck.

"As long as it takes to do what?"

So many questions! Could the man not see how distracted she was? She forced her gaze to his eyes. "As long as it takes to anticipate our vows, decide we will not suit, then dissolve the understanding."

He arched a brow. "We are going to end our

engagement based upon the realization that we will not suit?"

"Yes."

"A realization we will arrive at after anticipating our vows?"

"Yes." Now *she* crossed her arms. "Why do you sound so perturbed?"

"I sound perturbed because I am." He threw his arms out in a display of frustration. "This idea is just as poorly thought out as your original, and look how that turned out. No." He held up a hand as she drew breath to counter. "Do not say a word until I am done. No one will believe we have decided we 'do not suit.' No one. Not after what Lady Palmer and her entourage witnessed."

"They witnessed nothing but the sight of me sitting astride your lap."

"I told you to say nothing until I finished."

"Yes, well, I do not take kindly to orders."

He visibly ground his teeth together. "You might recall, I voiced my eagerness to continue our interrupted rendezvous with Lady Palmer and the others as witnesses—"

"Of course I recall. It was only last evening."

Now she could see and hear his teeth gnashing together. "*And,*" he went on as if she had not spoken, "in so doing, revealed my desire to be with you. Why, in God's name, would I decide *not* to be with you once securing your hand in marriage and your delectable person in my bed?"

"Perhaps it is I who finds you unsuitable? Perhaps I discover you are not as skill—"

"That will not work."

Eirene huffed. It was childish, but it seemed more mature than stomping her foot. "Why will *that not work*? Are you worried I will sully your rakish reputation? Compromise the success of future conquests? Or maybe—"

"No." The force behind that one word silenced her. "None of the above. It will not work because if you publicly decry my inability to please you in bed, you will have a line of men stretching from your front door to the bloody English Channel who are eager to succeed where I could not, increasing your current dilemma tenfold."

"Oh."

"Oh?"

"Yes. Oh." She turned her back on him. It really was easier to think when not looking directly at him. She stared into the fire until her eyes began to burn. "If finding fault with one another's performance in bed will not work"—she twisted her hands together—"what do you suggest we do?"

"You could actually marry me."

She closed her eyes and dug her nails into her palms to counter the unwanted longing his words aroused. "I cannot."

Why would he even suggest such a thing? He could not possibly wish to marry her. They barely knew one another. He was a rake, she a recluse. It would never work, regardless. No. It was entirely ludicrous.

"Eirene, look at me." He stood before her, blocking the fire. "Will you consider it?"

She shook her head. "I am sorry, but—"

"Say no more. For varied reasons your plan will not work, and for reasons unbeknownst to me, my suggestion is not acceptable, therefore, I would advise you to leave London as soon as possible, return to the country, and do your best to ignore any future advances you might deem unacceptable or inconvenient."

She stared at him for several moments, wondering if one last kiss would be appropriate. No. Best not to add to the memories already guaranteed to haunt the rest of her days.

"It seems this entire endeavor was doomed to fail from the beginning. Had I known my only remaining option would be to return to the country and simply ignore the unwanted advances of gentlemen, I would have remained in the country and avoided this useless trip to London. I could have done without the congestion, noise, and *smell*."

"Surely, it was not all bad?"

"Every moment of it." She turned away before he could react to the lie. Her grandfather had always told her anger was a powerful weapon but to wield it with great caution lest it inflict irreparable damage to its target. If Adrien thought of her in anger, he would forget her, and she needed to believe he would forget her.

"You should go, Eirene." The chill behind his word seeped directly into her skin.

She rubbed her cold flesh through the long, thin sleeves of her gown. Without looking back at him, she headed for the door. The urge to say something, *anything*, nearly overwhelmed her, but she managed to open the door and step into the corridor before doing or saying anything that might leave *her* irreparably damaged.

It was not until she was back in the privacy of her

own home, within the confines of her bedroom, that she allowed herself to cry. It was not an indulgence that lasted long. Crying, her grandfather always said, had the power to change nothing. To regret was a waste of time and a show of weakness. If one had better strategized, there would be no need to look back and wonder what if.

She had not strategized well in regards to Adrien. Not at all.

"You would not be proud of me at this moment, Grandfather. I have allowed myself to become weak, to give in to the very passions you so often warned against."

"My lady?" Hamish stood at the door making a poor attempt to hide his curiosity.

Eirene swiped at the last of her tears. "Pay no attention, Hamish, I merely indulged in a moment of emotional weakness, which has now ended."

"Of course, my lady. I did not mean to intrude, but I was curious how your visit with his lordship went. Has he agreed to your new plan? Will we be remaining in London a tad longer?"

"No and no." She moved to her vanity to peer at her tear-streaked face. No wonder Hamish wore an ill-disguised expression of horror. She looked a fright. Fresh air would do her good. It cured all ills, according to her grandfather, who had enjoyed a brisk walk at the beginning and end of every day, no matter the weather.

"I am going to take a walk, Hamish. In my absence, have the servants begin making preparations for our return to the country."

"Of course, my lady. Shall I ring for one of the footmen to accompany you?"

"I only mean to take a quick turn about the block. No need for an escort." She left her room, Hamish following on her heels.

Once in the foyer, he opened the door and waited while she buttoned her spencer and pulled on a pair of light weight gloves. The air coming in through the open door was brisk, and she longed to feel the chill in her bones. Perhaps it would numb the feeling she'd had since walking out of Adrien's bedroom.

One could only hope.

Chapter Twelve

Adrien fumed as he exited the house and headed for the mews. After Eirene's unexpected visit and the unsatisfactory conclusion of said visit, he needed a good long, hard ride to clear his mind, calm his temper, and extinguish his lust. Focused on the way she had oh-so-calmly walked out of his room, and possibly his life, he was not paying attention when he rounded the corner and stepped blindly into a well-placed fist.

The hit split his lower lip and knocked him to the ground. He barely got a hand out in time to break the fall, then regretted it when his wrist bent at a damned painful angle. Unsure if he should see to his bleeding lip, his throbbing jaw, or his tweaked wrist, he ignored all three and looked up from his prone position upon the ground.

"Sam? What the hell?"

Cyril's cousin reached down, yanked him to his feet, then slammed him against the uneven bricks of the nearest wall. The breath whooshed from Adrien's lungs, and stars filled his vision. He attempted to make a fist, but his hand had gone numb.

"I warned you," Sam hissed. He drew back and landed another solid punch to Adrien's jaw. The hit would have knocked him back on his arse if not for the arm Sam had locked across his chest. "I told you to stay away from her."

The next punch landed just below the ribs. The pain was extraordinary, enough so that he forgot all about the numbness of his hand and the likely damage to his wrist. He had not been in a full out fisticuffs since university. He'd won that confrontation, but he did not like his chances presently. He couldn't even get a leg up to knee Sam in the stones. Their bodies were pressed together, chest to thigh, Sam using his full weight to keep Adrien pinned.

"Christ, Sam, leave off." Adrien groped for the sleeve of Sam's coat in an attempt to be free from the manacle of his forearm. His efforts were rewarded with another bruising punch to the ribs. A burning pain followed the hit and grew worse with each breath he took.

Damn. The bastard had cracked a rib. Or two.

"I still plan to marry her, you know." Sam panted like a crazed dog while landing a few more punches to his side. One glanced off his hip bone, sending a wave of numbness down his leg. "It don't matter if she's whored for you."

"Go near her, and I will kill you." Adrien spoke through his teeth as he fought against the pain roaring through his body. Eirene had made it perfectly clear she did not want to be a part of his life, but damned if he would allow Sam to force her to be a part of his.

"You can try," Sam snarled in Adrien's face, "but I think you'll find yourself too busy with other matters to care what becomes of Lady Rowe-Weston."

"What does that—" Before he could finish, Sam ripped him away from the wall, kneed him in the groin, landed another punch directly to his jaw, then tossed him in the gutter where he proceeded to grind a boot heel into his damaged ribs.

Mere de Dieu!

"Consider this your last day among polite society, *peasant*." For good measure, Sam dug his heel in deeper, then spit in Adrien's face before stalking away.

Adrien listened to the sound of Sam's retreating steps as his vision swam and his mouth filled with blood. He rolled his head to allow the blood to dribble to the cobbles so as not to choke to death.

Bloody hell, Sam had become a madman. He belonged in Bedlam, not roaming the streets threatening to force wealthy spinsters into marriage. Unsuspecting spinsters. Yes, he had warned Eirene about Sam's intentions, but she had not appeared overly concerned. The vexing woman probably believed herself too well trained by her sainted grandfather to become anyone's victim. Well, she was wrong. Sam would not rest until he possessed her wealth.

Any doubts Adrien might have harbored to the contrary had been pummeled out of him. He needed to warn her, and this time she needed to listen.

But first he had to get himself out of the gutter.

He rolled back and forth in a wasted effort to gain enough momentum to propel himself to his feet. Winded, he ceased the rocking and gazed up at the gray sky. Tears burned his eyes. Brought on by the sharp smell of whatever offal he'd landed in, no doubt. If any of his acquaintances were to see him now, they'd believe he cried over the damage done to his coat. Though given Sam's not so subtle threat, come morning, his acquaintances would know the truth. Benoit, the vicomte known for his dashing good taste and prowess with women and cards, would be no more.

He might as well remain in the stinking gutter.
****

Eirene, having completed her brisk turn about the block, paused a moment before taking the final turn, which would lead her home. A twinge of unease skittered up her spine, and she looked behind her, but there was no one and nothing. Her grandfather had always cautioned against ignoring the body's attempts to sound a warning. One did not feel uneasy without cause, he would say.

Despite Adrien and Mister Westhaven's dire warnings and the sage advice of her grandfather, she ignored the brief moment of unease. She very much doubted Lord Petley would accost her in broad daylight. Assuming he meant to accost her at all. She simply could not imagine the man so desperate for her fortune he would take such extreme risks with his reputation or that of his younger sister's.

Adrien disagreed, but then, she and Adrien disagreed on much. Never before had that been more evident than when he had shocked her senseless with a marriage proposal. What could he have been thinking? Had she not made her stance on marriage perfectly clear? Did he truly believe a few mind-shattering kisses would alter her opinion?

"Ha. Men and their arrogance," she mumbled while gathering her hem to continue on her way. "It would take a great deal more than seductive caresses to convince me to marry."

"I do believe a gun might do the trick, my lady." The threatening voice accompanied the feel of a hard object pressed against her lower back. "No, no, do not turn around and do not attempt to scream for help."

"Lord Petley, I presume?" So much for her believing the man too sane to attempt such a bold maneuver.

"At your service." He pressed close to her side, his cheek lowering to brush against hers. From the corner of her eye, she registered his dark coloring. "I have a carriage just around the corner. I suggest you do nothing that might force me to pull this trigger."

Eirene halted and turned to confront Petley head on. Her initial impression of his looks was favorable. In fact, he seemed quite handsome enough to secure a willing participant in the institution of marriage. Were guns really necessary?

"Do you always follow directions so poorly, my lady?" He had no choice but to tuck the pistol into his jacket lest it draw notice.

"I rather doubt you actually intend to shoot me. What would be the point? If it is my money you covet. My dead body would greatly hinder your quest. So kindly put that toy away and let us discuss this like two adults, hmm?" She crossed her arms and waited.

Looking as if he wished to shoot her multiple times, Petley scowled at her logic and crammed the pistol into the back of his trousers. "Rumor has it you're an unnatural woman, and for once, it seems the gossips were correct."

"Not unnatural, simply logical. Now, what is it you want from me, my lord?"

"I want every last shilling of your fortune." He possessed incredibly dark eyes, so dark, the iris nearly matched the pupil.

Eirene refused to allow the man's raven-like eyes to unnerve her. "That is unfortunate, my lord, for I've no intention of giving you a single shilling."

He stepped closer, forcing her to back against a neatly maintained hedgerow. "At one time you must have been willing to give me something, hmm? Why else send an invitation asking me to meet privately with you?"

"You were one of five men to rec—"

"Oh, aye, I am well aware of the others, and I had thought I'd made it perfectly clear it was in their best interests to drop out of the competition. Sadly, a certain Frenchman proved a tad stubborn, but I believe he has been shown the error of his ways after our little meeting this afternoon." He flexed his right hand, drawing her attention to his bare skin. His knuckles were smeared with blood. "That's right," he sneered, following her gaze to his hand. "That is your lover's blood."

Eirene's heart thumped painfully as she dragged her gaze back to Petley's face. The man did not have a mark on him, as if Adrien had been unable to defend himself. My God, had Petley attacked from behind? Or had he simply shot Adrien without warning?

"I left him alive," Petley said in response to her unasked question. "Killing him would have been too easy and would have denied me the pleasure of watching him fall into ruin."

She frowned at that. "What did you do?"

"Besides rearrange his ribs and mar his pretty face? You will have to wait for tomorrow's paper, for I refuse to ruin the surprise." Despite the darkness of his eyes, they managed to glint with triumph.

In that moment, she knew. Petley knew of Adrien's secret, and come morning, all of London would know as well. How Petley was in possession of such

Lora Darling

knowledge, she had no idea, but she would stake her life that was precisely what the cad had done. She would also stake a goodly portion of her wealth that Adrien would see the article and believe her to be the source. After all, he had confessed she and Cyril to be the only ones privy to the truth and she doubted he would ever suspect his dear friend, Cyril.

No, he would blame her. And then he would despise her for it.

That alone was reason enough to attempt to wrestle Petley for his pistol so that she might put a bullet in the fiend's gut. How dare he orchestrate such a disaster? What right did he have and how did he believe it would somehow lead to the acquisition of her bloody fortune?

She asked as much.

"I do not have to explain my actions to you." He glanced both directions then took firm hold of her arm. "I might not shoot you here and now, my lady, but I strongly suggest you cooperate and allow me to escort you to my carriage."

"Or what?" She struggled to pull her arm free, but Lord Petley was a rather tall, strong male specimen.

"Take a look across the street and tell me what you see, my lady?"

The command was so unexpected it took her a moment to process it and obey. "What am I supposed to—" She bit off the rest of the question as her gaze zeroed in on the one thing that did not belong amongst the Georgian architecture. The rough looking man doffed his cap upon noticing her regard.

"If I give the signal, he will enter your home and kill your staff."

Eirene tore her gaze from the ruffian across the

164

street and stared in horror at Lord Petley. "Why are you doing this?"

"It is rather simple, really." He began to lead her down the walkway. "I find myself in great need of your wealth, and I mean to have it."

For the sake of Hamish and the rest of her staff, she hiked up her hem and kept stride with Petley. His carriage awaited them around the corner, and as he opened the door and shoved her inside, she did nothing to thwart him. He climbed in after and slammed the door. As he banged on the ceiling to order the driver to go, she stared out the window and began to strategize an escape.

****

The patter of footsteps echoed up and down the alley, rousing Adrien to semi-consciousness. They drew closer, and before he could attempt to lift his head, the steps halted and deft hands flitted across his body. He swatted as best he could, but there seemed to be dozens of fingers.

"Leaf off, damn it." His command carried a lisp as he forced the words past his throbbing lip.

The hands stilled but did not vanish. "Bloke's not dead. Be quick, lads."

On the heels of that order, Adrien was aware of a hand rooting deep into his waistcoat to relieve him of his watch. Another hand fumbled at the waist band of his trousers. Bloody hell, did they mean to strip him bare all while he lay helpless as a beached fish? A shrill whistle rang out from the end of the alley, and the hands and the bodies they were attached to scattered like a flock of crows.

Heavy footsteps approached. "Monsieur?"

Adrien rolled his head and blinked toward the figure crouched by his side. Red hair. Hard jaw. Hooded eyes. Wild brows. "Hamish?"

"Aye." Eirene's butler frowned heavily as he swept his gaze along Adrien's prone form. "Those ruffians worked you over g—"

"No. It wasn't them." Adrien attempted to push his weight onto his elbows, but his ribs would have none of it. *Mere de Dieu*! Had they moved? Had his ribs actually *moved*? He fell back with a sickening thwack of his skull against cobbles.

"Easy, *monsieur*, you'll do my ladyship no good if you stain this alley with your brains."

"Your ladyship?" Somewhere amidst the fog of pain, his mind began to piece together the obvious. Hamish, Eirene's butler, was at his side, looking as if he'd been running from the devil. *Why?*

"I'll spare you the need to ask, your lordship. He took her, he did. To the casual observer it weren't a kidnapping, but I know what I saw and I know my lady. She'd not go with the likes of him. Not willingly."

"What?" Adrien fought against the pain and managed to shift most of his weight upon his left elbow. The alley spun behind Hamish, but he fixed his gaze on the man's light brown eyes and ignored the tilting world. "What are you saying?"

"My lady has been kidnapped."

Eirene. Kidnapped. "When?"

Hamish shook his head. "Not more than an hour ago. I'd have been quicker if I hadn't wasted time trying to hail a cab. Decided just to hoof it instead, but you weren't in. Butler said you'd gone for a ride, suggested I check the mews, seeing as how he figured you might have returned. So I did." He spread his hands and arched a brow. "I guess you returned."

"No. I never went on the damn ride." Adrien glanced at the sky and the position of the sun. It hung low, an indication he'd been lying in the gutter far too long. "Help me up, Hamish."

He extended his left hand—his right still lacked feeling—and did what he could to aid Hamish in the task of pulling him to his feet. If Eirene's butler noticed the moisture on Adrien's face or the gasps of pain punctuating each shallow breath, he gave no indication.

Cyril nearly dropped dead upon seeing Adrien as Hamish all but carried him into the house. "My God! What the devil happened? Did Chevalier throw you?"

Adrien shook his head and extracted himself from Hamish's supportive body. "Thank you, my good man. Lady Rowe-Weston is lucky to have you in her employ."

"Speaking of my lady, my lord—"

Adrien held up a hand to silence the butler, then gave his attention to Cyril. "Chev did not throw me. I was attacked on my way to the mews." At least he could now speak without lisping or spitting blood all over the place.

"Attacked? I'll have the ruffians hanged, I will!" Cyril drew a great breath as if to yell for Bow Street right then and there.

"It was Sam who attacked me, Cyril."

Cyril's mouth slammed shut with enough force to vibrate the loose skin about his jaw line. "Sam? Why the devil would Sam attack you in the mews? Are you quite certain? Is it—"

"I am, without a shadow of a doubt, certain as to

the identity of my attacker. He did not merely throw punches. He also announced his intentions to wed Lady Rowe-Weston, whether the lady agreed or not—"

"He'll take her to Gretna, he will," Hamish put in, earning a confused look from Cyril. "Begging your pardon, sir, but your cousin took my lady. 'Tis why I was racing to reach his lordship. I thought perhaps the viscount—"

"As to that," Adrien interrupted with a painful sigh, "Sam means to expose me."

Cyril gaped at Adrien. "Expose you? You mean—"

"Oui." Standing had become rather taxing for Adrien of a sudden, and he found himself swaying toward Hamish. The butler caught him before he could crash to the floor in a pile of indignity.

"Perhaps we should adjourn to the parlor?" Cyril led the way, glancing over his shoulder every half step to ensure Hamish was handling Adrien with care. It took a lifetime, but finally, Adrien was ensconced in a comfortable chair, his feet propped upon a low stool. "Is that better?" Cyril hovered like a nursemaid. "Would you like a drink?"

"I would very much appreciate a drink."

Cyril flitted away to see to the request, then returned with a lovely measure of whiskey, which Adrien drank without giving a moment's consideration to his split lip. He nearly threw the glass into the hearth as the sting of alcohol set his injured mouth on fire.

"Mere de Dieu!" He lowered the glass to his thigh and dropped his head back in the chair.

"At least the wound is now clean," Hamish offered.

"Quite," Cyril agreed.

Adrien stared at the ceiling and moaned. "If you

two are through, perhaps we should return to the small matter of Lord Petley's nefarious deeds."

The chair opposite creaked, indicating Cyril had taken a seat.

Adrien lifted his head to meet his friend's gaze. "I'll go after them, of course."

"The hell you will. You can't ride in your current state. You're mad to even cons—"

"I will go after her." Adrien glanced at Hamish who remained standing. "An hour, you said?"

"Give or take, my lord."

Adrien returned his attention to Cyril. "Chevalier will have no trouble overtaking them."

"Aye, especially after you fall from the saddle and he leaves you behind." Cyril sat forward. "You cannot be serious, Adrien. You're moving about like a man with broken ribs. How can you spend any time in a saddle? What good will you do Lady Rowe-Weston if you do irreversible damage to your insides?"

"Dammit, Cyril, what choice do I have?"

"You could send someone in your stead? Westhaven is a good chap. Send him. Or Venton. That devil would love a reason to stomp Sam into the ground after their disagreement at the track last year."

"Disagreement?" Adrien shook his head and cautiously took a sip of whiskey. The sting was not quite so bad. "Sam cheated and Venton lost a fortune. No, if given the slightest motive, Venton will put a bullet in your cousin and you can't possibly want that."

"No." Cyril sat back with a defeated sigh. "He is proving himself to be quite a foul creature, but I've no wish to have him murdered."

"Then it is settled." Adrien drained the rest of his

drink, then attempted to push to his feet. Hamish rushed forward to help, but he waved him away. After a few steadying breaths, he managed to gain his feet. His ribs protested in earnest, nearly sending him back into the chair.

"You'll need your ribs bound if you mean to ride, my lord."

Adrien nodded at Hamish, too busy concentrating on not passing out to manage more.

"Are you adept at such things, man?" Cyril demanded, and when Hamish indicated he was, Cyril rang for Sayers. "My man will see that you have what you need." Then to Adrien, he said, "I still think you are mad to ride after them."

Adrien spread his hands. "Cyril, I—"

"Yes, yes, I know. You love her." There was no mistaking Cyril's tone.

"You do not approve."

Cyril retook his seat. They were alone now, Hamish having gone out to confer with Sayers. "It is not my place to approve or disapprove, but have you told her how you feel?"

"Oui."

"And?"

"She wants nothing to do with marriage."

Cyril's eyes widened. "You *proposed*?"

"I did. She said no, and that, as they say, is that."

"Yet you intend to risk your well-being going after her. Why? What is there to gain?"

"Must I gain anything? Can I not simply wish to see her safe?" Adrien shifted his focus to the fire. "Is that not the true definition of love, Cyril?"

"Aye, I imagine it is."

Chapter Thirteen

Eirene glared at Lord Petley across the dim interior of his carriage. Her hands lay atop her lap, tied together with silk cord. Initially, he had stuffed a handkerchief in her mouth, but he had removed it mere moments ago with a stern order for her to hold her tongue or she'd find the cloth stuffed down her throat once more. She did not doubt him. There was a disturbing darkness beneath Lord Samuel Petley's handsome exterior. It promised unpredictability and hinted at a character lacking in remorse. Her grandfather would have referred to Petley as unhinged. An apt description and one that warned her to tread lightly.

"If you've something to say, say it. Your staring grows tedious."

There were a great many things she could say to the man, but most of them would only incite his temper, and she had no way to escape if he decided to lash out physically. Thus far, he'd not done a thing to hurt her. She would like to keep it that way.

"Where are we going?" It seemed an innocent enough question.

"Gretna Green."

"I see." Dear God. She had suspected as much, given the direction they were headed and the number of hours they had been on the road, but hearing him admit his intentions made the situation alarmingly real. She forced herself to chuckle. "And here I had always believed ladies were only kidnapped and hauled off to Gretna Green within the pages of horrid novels."

"You thought wrong. Now shut your mouth, or I'll gag you again." Petley slouched upon his bench with his hat tugged low over his eyes. The carriage hit a rather jarring rut, and he swore under his breath then banged a gloved fist against the ceiling.

"Beggin' your pardon, my lord," the driver called. "'Tis getting hard to see. Shall we put up for the night?"

Petley grunted while palming his watch. He snapped open the face, scowled, then barked at the driver to pull off at the next inn. Shoving the watch back into its pocket, he tapped his hat brim and exposed his eyes in order to glare at Eirene. "One wrong move or word from you and your night will become very uncomfortable. Understand?"

She nodded, thinking it wiser to remain silent. Plus, silence allowed her to think. It was rather obvious she had to escape Petley's company, lest she end up married to the man. The inn would provide the best opportunity, but she would have to play her cards wisely. Men such as Petley did not play the fool twice. If her attempt failed, she might find herself lashed to the carriage roof or worse. She need only be *conscious* to speak wedding vows.

Petley shifted to the edge of his bench and reached for her. It took a moment for him to untie the silk knots, but finally, she was free. She shook her hands, then winced at the sudden return of blood to her fingers. Ignoring the tingling, she closed and opened her hands into fists.

"We will secure a room as husband and wife, and

you'll say nothing to the contrary, understand?" He grunted in approval when she nodded in understanding. "Good. I was hoping you were smart enough to see reason. I would hate to do any damage to your lovely face or form, and don't think I wouldn't."

Eirene averted her gaze from the man across the aisle and looked out the window. The night beyond was dark and thick with fog. "Where are we?"

"No idea." Offering nothing further on the matter, Petley resumed his slouch, crossed his arms, and dipped his chin to once more hide beneath the brim of his hat.

"Why are you doing this?"

Petley cocked his head in order to stare at her with one eye, its black iris absorbing the meager light from the swaying carriage lantern. "Come now, Lady Rowe-Weston, I informed you of my reasons."

"You want my money."

"And I will have it." He sat up and leaned forward with his elbows resting on his knees and his direct stare unnervingly steady. "I had hoped it would not come to this, but you left me no choice. If only you had permitted me to call, we might have had a normal courtship."

"I did not come to London to be courted, Lord Petley."

He sat back and crossed his arms. "Why did you come to London?"

Eirene shifted her gaze out the window once more. "*That* is none of your concern."

"Perhaps not, but there is something that greatly concerns me and that is your relationship with Benoit."

She turned sharply to look at him. "I have no relationship with Vicomte Benoit."

He tsked and shook his head. "You are attempting to play stupid again, my lady, and it is not an act that suits you. Now answer the question. What is between you and Benoit?"

"Nothing beyond a foolish moment of passion, which I instantly regretted."

"Is that so?" He studied her for a few moments, then slowly smiled. "Why, then, did you feel the need to pay him a visit this morning? Hmm? A rather lengthy visit, I might add."

"Were you following me?" Her skin grew cold at the thought of being stalked like prey.

"Let us just say I was keeping an eye on Benoit." He waved his hand. "But, please, you were about to explain the reason for your visit."

Obviously, she could not tell him the truth, that she'd gone to Adrien to propose a faux engagement. "To be honest, my reason is rather humiliating."

She looked away and affected what she hoped was a reasonably convincing expression of shame.

"Come, my lady, do not turn shy now. After all, you are to be my bride."

The words turned Eirene's stomach. "I went to him in a moment of weakness"—she lowered her voice— "to see if the things he said to me at Lady Palmer's were true. They were not." She looked across the aisle. "So, I assure you, there is nothing between Lord Benoit and myself and never will be." Saying the words aloud caused a shocking degree of pain.

"Is that so?" Petley once more leaned forward in order to search every inch of her face with his fathomless, dark eyes. "Let us assume for a moment you are lying, hmm? No, no, play along, my lady. If you still carry a torch for Benoit, there are a few things you should be made aware of. For starters, he is not whom he claims to be."

She had no idea if it would be to her benefit or detriment to admit she knew the truth about Adrien, so she remained silent and schooled her features.

"In fact," Petley continued, in an oh-so-self-satisfied tone. "He is nothing but a commoner, a blacksmith's son." He glanced at his knuckles, which displayed a smattering of bruises. "There was nothing blue about his blood." He winked at her.

"You wasted your time hurting the monsieur. He truly wants nothing to do with me."

"One can never be too careful, my lady, and I needed to make certain Adrien understood the lay of the land." The carriage rolled to a stop, causing Petley to shift his gaze out the window. Eirene did the same and saw they had arrived at the coaching inn. It was a large, white-washed, square structure with narrow, black-shuttered windows and a sagging roof. A weathered sign swung above the door declaring, The Devil's Inn, est. 1456.

"Charming," Petley murmured before throwing open the coach door and jumping down onto the gravel. He pitched slightly forward as if thrown off balance, then swore under his breath.

The driver appeared over his shoulder. "Easy, your lordship," he warned while placing a steadying hand upon Petley's shoulder. "These stones haven't seen a rake in God knows how long. You'll be needing to watch your step."

"Yes, quite." Petley shrugged off the man's hand, then reached inside toward Eirene. "Do not dawdle, my dear." He squeezed her fingers and all but pulled her from the coach. The uneven gravel shifted beneath her walking boots, adding weight to the driver's keen warning.

Petley tucked her hand around his elbow, then turned to the driver. "See to the horses, and if this place has a decent pair, switch them out. I trust your assessment of the matter."

"Aye, my lord." The man doffed his hat and strolled away. It did not take long for him to vanish into the thick shadows.

Eirene looked about the courtyard. The torch burning alongside the inn door and the two posts marking the entrance to the yard did little to illuminate the vast space. She shivered with unease. Anyone or any*thing* could emerge from the darkness without a lick of warning.

Petley moved forward, giving her a little tug to ensure she kept pace. "No doubt you are accustomed to more elaborate lodgings, but we paupers must make do." He shot her a scathing look that even the darkness around them could not hide.

She hiked up her skirts with her free hand and lengthened her stride. He was a tall man with very long legs. "For a pauper, you play the part of a wealthy lord to perfection."

He halted without warning, causing her to almost stroll right by him. "Do you have any idea what would become of me if my lack of financial stability were to become public?"

"There is no shortage of financially pressed gentlemen cavorting about London, Lord Petley. You would hardly be shunned." He acted as if the only thing standing between life and death was his faux wealth.

"You know nothing." He pivoted on his boot heels and began walking again, pulling her along at his side. "My sister's debut would fail before it had a chance to happen. She would be labeled a treasure seeker and forced to settle for a man twice her age and burdened with children." He shot her a glare. "I'll not have my sister suffer a loveless marriage to a man more in need of a governess than a wife."

"Yet you have no qualms about forcing *me* into a loveless match."

"This marriage will only last as long as it takes to transfer your wealth into my name."

If he hadn't had a hold of her, she would have stopped dead in her tracks. Had he just insinuated what it sounded like? Did he mean to marry her, take control of her wealth, then dispose of her? By what means? Death? An asylum? A dark attic? If given a choice, the former seemed the most merciful. God help her.

The inside of the inn was just as dark and unwelcoming as the yard. The ceiling sagged in places, as if tired of bearing the weight of the rooms above, and the floor pitched and heaved, as if the planks had been laid over freshly dug graves. She stepped lightly, fearful of what might lay underfoot as well as the possibility a bed might come crashing down upon her head at any moment. Cautious maneuvering proved a difficult task considering the tables and chairs canted at odd angles in deference to the uneven flooring. Sidestepping one meant knocking into the next, which sent up a thick plume of dust so foul her eyes watered and her throat burned.

Perhaps the date on the sign also indicated the last

time a broom had been employed.

They reached the low counter built into the back wall of the establishment. A low-burning lantern hung on a nearby pillar, illuminating a young girl with a bruised eye, lank, dirty-blond hair, and surprisingly pretty features. She scowled as they approached.

"We need a room," Petley announced without preamble. "Your best."

Eirene almost laughed. A public mews would likely put this place to shame.

"I suppose you be expectin' a hot meal as well, yer lordship?" the girl asked the question while plunking a very large key on the counter, followed by a covered taper, which she lit with shaking, scarred hands. The glass rattled dangerously as she slid it back over the flame.

"If you have anything decent to eat in this establishment, yes."

"Oh, aye, we do. Folks come from all over for our meat pies, they do."

Eirene glanced back at the very empty taproom. Perhaps they had missed this evening's rush of hungry patrons.

"Yes, that sounds fine. And a decent ale if you have it." Petley took the key in one hand while tossing a few coins upon the counter with the other. "My lady will require the services of a maid, and a hot bath would be most welcome."

Good lord, was Petley blind? They'd be lucky to find an empty chamber pot in their room, let alone a hot bath and a lady's maid.

The girl chortled and slid a glance in Eirene's direction. "Can't your fancy man unlace you, my lady?"

Her snide remark earned her the sting of Petley's backhand. Eirene could not have said which of them was more shocked by his actions, her or the girl. Blinking back tears, the girl ducked her head and mumbled an apology before declaring herself the only servant available.

"Then I suggest you get busy filling buckets." Snatching up the candle, Petley stalked toward the narrow staircase, pausing to look back as he reached the bottom. "My lady?"

Eirene attempted to catch the servant's eye, but the girl scurried out from behind the counter and vanished through a swinging door. With no other choice, Eirene gathered her skirts and followed Petley. He held the candle aloft, though its flickering flame offered little to no illumination. In addition to the lack of light, the stairs pitched sharply to the left, making for a precarious journey to the top. The narrow, low-ceilinged corridor was no better, though Petley walked with his shoulders back and chin up as though traversing the floorboards of a grand palace.

She added delusional to his list of faults, which already included arrogant, unpredictable, and after his behavior toward the girl, violent.

Their room was located at the end of the corridor and up a short flight of stairs. It was large, cold, filthy, and foul smelling, and she was grateful for the pathetic glow of the candle lest a brighter light reveal things best left unseen. Hoping for a bit of fresh air, she moved to one of the two leaded glass windows, but it refused to open. The other proved just as stubborn. Wonderful.

"Allow me." Petley nudged her aside and managed to open the window a scant two inches before it stuck.

The powerful smell of manure and horse wafted into the room.

Clasping her hand over nose and mouth, Eirene gagged. "Perhaps we should reconsider the wisdom of spending the night?"

Petley turned and propped a hip against the sill. "If you are so eager to become my bride, I see no reason to wait for the vows." He pushed away from the window and stalked toward her. "I'm not keen to have Benoit's leavings, but for you, I shall make an exception."

Eirene backed up until her legs hit the hard frame of the bed. "Do not touch me."

Laughing, he reached her in two strides and latched onto her arms with a bruising grip. "You put on such airs for someone who spread her legs for the son of a blacksmith." He yanked her against his body and lowered his head.

Eirene twisted away from the descent of his mouth. "We cannot. *I* cannot." She looked him in the eye. "I am indisposed, my lord."

He released her, as if she had claimed to have the plague. "A convenient excuse, but how do I know it is true?"

"If it is proof you require…" She gathered fistfuls of her skirt and began to lift it. As the material rose to knee height, Petley blanched and held up his hands in surrender. Relieved that he had fallen for the ruse, she dropped her gown and smoothed out the wrinkles.

"No matter, your lack of virginity plays in my favor. Whether I touch you or not, your body will show proof of consummation, rendering our marriage legal and most binding."

Sound reasoning if not for one minor flaw. Her

virginity was still very much intact, giving her a weapon she would not hesitate to employ.

****

Adrien tightened his hold on the reins in order to coax Chevalier down to a trot. It frustrated him they had not seen a hint of Petley's carriage, let alone overtaken it as he believed they might, but he'd been pushing his faithful stallion hard for hours and would do neither of them any favors by keeping to the punishing pace. The horse needed to rest, and he needed to give his ribs a break from the painful jarring. Besides, it had become too dark to safely continue without fear of misstep. He'd never forgive himself if Chev came up lame.

The road ahead offered no clear pull off, so he merely guided Chev onto the grass and under a large, heavy-limbed tree. The horse snorted and tossed his head, excited by the much needed moment of rest.

"Easy, boy," Adrien cooed. He slid his hand under the thick, black mane to check for signs that he'd pushed his mount too hard, but the quivering flesh was devoid of lather. Giving Chev a hearty pat, he swung a leg over the front of the saddle to dismount. His ribs protested the jarring impact of his feet hitting the ground, but after a few shallow breaths, the pain eased.

Turning his attention to securing Chevalier, he tossed the reins over a low branch and went to work removing saddle and blanket. Chev gave a mighty ripple of relief as the weight was lifted from his back.

"Enjoy while you can, my friend. We can't rest for long." Adrien set the saddle at the base of the tree, covered it with the blanket, and took a seat against it. He stretched out his legs and lifted his arms over his head to work out the kinks that came from being in the saddle for an extended time. The movement did his ribs no favors, but he ignored the pain. He'd come to the conclusion that nothing was broken, and he was fairly certain no one had ever died from a bruised rib. It was too important that he find Eirene to allow a bit of pain to stop him.

Completing the stretch, he drew up his knees and lowered his arms to cross them over his chest. How far had Sam and Eirene managed to travel in the last eight or so hours? It would be days before they reached Gretna, and he had no doubt that was Sam's intended destination. Assuming they put up for the night, if for no other reason than to rest the horses, Chev should overtake them at some point. Plus, there was the fact Sam was traveling with a woman and concessions had to be made for her comfort. Hell, if luck were on Adrien's side, perhaps Sam would decide to spend an entire night at a coaching inn—

"Mere de Dieu," Adrien cursed as the unthinkable filtered into his mind. If Sam laid a single finger on Eirene, he would pay dearly for it. Though knowing Eirene, she no doubt believed herself perfectly capable of handling anything Petley might throw her way. But unless the woman had armed herself before taking her ill-advised stroll, she would find herself at a severe disadvantage. Petley was the sort of aggressor who would not stop until the fight was won. He was a wild boar intent upon charging until someone put a bullet between its eyes.

God willing, it would not come to that. Adrien had no desire to shoot Cyril's cousin. In fact, he had vowed not to. But Cyril had to realize, Eirene's safety trumped

Petley's well-being. After all, she was the woman Adrien loved. Whether she ever accepted his affection or not, it did not change his need to see her safe. If she wished to live out her days secluded in the country, *c'est la vie*. He would respect whatever decision she made, but not before he laid his heart bare one last time.

But first he had to find her.

Chevalier chose that moment to toss his head and dance in place. The stallion's agitation brought Adrien to his feet. Running a hand along the horse's side, he cooed softly, but Chevalier refused to settle.

"What is it, boy?" Adrien searched the darkness. The sliver of a moon offered little to no illumination, but he'd had hours to acclimate his eyes to the night. He saw nothing. Whatever had spooked Chev, likely a rabbit or fox, had moved on. And they should do the same.

"Sorry, boy, but our rest is over." Replacing the saddle proved a tad more difficult in the dark, but familiarity guided his hands, and after checking the cinch three times, he felt confident all was in order. With a deep, bracing breath, he swung up onto Chev's back and turned him toward the road. The stallion's steps were heavy, and he kept his head low. Adrien allowed the sluggish pace until Chev finally lifted his head, swiveled his ears, and blew out a loud breath.

Leaning forward over the horse's neck, Adrien stroked an ear. "Ready, boy?"

Chev tossed his head, tugging at the reins. All it took was a light kick of his heels and a loosening of the reins and Chev took off.

Chapter Fourteen

Eirene shot nervous glances over her shoulder toward the door as she prowled the room in search of a weapon. Petley had gone below stairs to check on the progress of their requested hot meal, allowing her a few blessed moments of privacy. She'd made quick work of the chamber pot and set about seeing to the task of arming herself for his return. Thus far the room had yielded nothing of use. Not even a fire poker.

Ready to give up, she scooted upon her hands and knees to look under the bed. How she would explain the condition of her clothing should Petley notice, she hadn't a clue, nor could she worry about that right now. She peered under the worn edge of the coverlet. The chamber pot might work, fashioned as it was from very heavy stoneware, but she would have to get within grabbing distance to wield it with enough force to knock Petley senseless and that gave him a chance to get his hands on her. He was a big man, and she would prefer a weapon that would keep her out of arm's reach.

"Blast!" She sat back upon her heels and let out a defeated sigh. To make matters worse, his return echoed beyond the door. Not bothering to get up, she met his gaze as he burst into the room.

"What the devil are you doing on the floor?" He carried a large wooden tray, laden with two covered plates.

"I had need of the chamber pot." Gathering her skirts, she climbed to her feet and did her best to shake off the majority of dust, though she had every intention of burning the outfit she wore. Until the end of days, it would remind her of Petley's ill intentions.

Assuming she managed to get free of him.

He kicked the door closed and stalked across the room to place the tray upon the small, round table situated close to the window. Not the most inviting location for a meal given the smell of the stables.

"Come eat." He whisked off the covers and took a deep breath. "Smells good."

It smelled like old boot to Eirene, but she kept the opinion to herself and slowly approached the table to take in the fare. Meat pies, or so she assumed. One was slightly larger and bulged unattractively.

Petley poked his fork into the larger pie, which expelled a great waft of steam and another whiff of old boot. He glanced at her. "Don't tell me you're too good to enjoy good country fare, my lady." Without waiting for her to join him, he filled his fork and shoveled the bite into his mouth. "Damn good," he declared while still chewing.

Eirene pressed a hand to her rolling stomach. She would rather starve. After saying as much, she left Petley to his meal and took a seat on the edge of the bed. While searching for a weapon, she had checked for bugs, surprised beyond all belief to find none in residence.

With Petley momentarily distracted, she allowed her mind to wander. Hamish would be beside himself with worry by now, of that she had no doubt. What would he do? She could not imagine the Scot engaging the services of Bow Street, but surely he would wish to locate his wayward mistress. If not Bow Street, where would he turn for help? She had no friends in London. Hell, she only had one acquaintance, if she chose to categorize Adrien as such.

Would Hamish appeal to Adrien for help?

The prospect of Adrien searching for her brought her hand against her stomach once more to quell the rolling. But it wasn't indigestion this time that tightened her gut. Her grandfather had trained her to be an independent woman. He would expect her to rectify her current, unfortunate situation on her own, and she believed the chance to do so would eventually present itself. However, she'd be lying if she claimed the thought of Adrien crashing through the door to affect a rescue did not thrill her. Surely, her grandfather would understand the difference between being helpless and wishing to be cared for.

The clatter of a fork drew her gaze toward the window. Petley stood hunched over the table, gripping the edge with enough force to turn his knuckles white. Both plates were empty, and she wondered if he had merely consumed the food too quickly, though that would not account for the ashen color of his complexion or the beads of sweat that rolled down his face. She stood, but before she could take a single step or speak a single word of inquiry, Petley toppled to the floor like a felled tree.

"My lord?" Eirene hurried to Petley but stopped short of kneeling at his side. His wide open eyes gazed up at her in pure agony while he pulled at the clothing over his stomach.

"Help me," he croaked just as a bubble of white

foam crested over his bottom lip.

"Oh my God." Eirene covered her mouth with a trembling hand, unsure what to do. Her grandfather had never taught her how to help a person who had been poisoned, he'd only taught her how to administer said poison.

Oh dear God. If Petley died, she would be blamed.

****

Chevalier threw a shoe an hour after Adrien had returned to the saddle. Cursing, he immediately reined the horse to a halt and jumped down. "It's all right, boy."

Adrien ran his hand down Chev's muzzle as the horse tossed his head and snorted in agitation. Once he'd gotten the large stallion calmed, he checked each leg for damage, then cradled Chev's right foreleg upon his thighs to inspect the hoof. From what he could ascertain, given the lack of light, the shoe had come off clean.

Placing the horse's foot back on the ground, he patted under Chev's mane. "You'll be fine, *mon ami*, but I guess we had better return to the inn we just passed, hmm?" Flipping the reins over Chev's ears, he coiled them around his fist and turned the horse about.

The inn had not looked at all inviting, with its poorly lit courtyard and sagging roof, and he had dismissed it as a likely place for Sam to stop. Petley, in spite of empty pockets, maintained very high standards and image was everything to the arrogant lord. No, Petley would have continued on with the hope of locating a much more inviting inn, but Adrien could not be as choosey. The rundown inn had boasted a stable, and where there was a stable, there would be horseshoes. Even if he had to do the job himself.

Aware of the precious time it was costing him, he walked Chevalier as fast as he deemed comfortable. When they reached the inn's courtyard, he breathed a sigh of relief and took in his surroundings. Proximity did not improve his impression of the place. In fact, it painted a much bleaker image. The roof not only sagged, it boasted a few holes large enough to allow copious amounts of rain to fall on any unsuspecting visitors unlucky enough to have taken an ill-placed room. In addition, the gravel under foot was sharp and unlevel. Chev tossed his head in protest as his unprotected hoof likely encountered an unfriendly shard of stone.

"The Devil's Inn," Adrien murmured while reading the sign. "How fitting." Thankfully, he did not need to pass the night inside the place. A quick trip to the stable and he should be back on the road in no time.

The stables were dark as pitch, but he could hear the scuff of hooves and the occasional huff of equine breath. Leaving Chev tethered outside, he stepped under the lintel and entered the dark, unwelcoming space. Light from a dying lantern, hanging low on a beam, did little to illuminate the interior, and the bulky shadow of a large carriage obstructed his view beyond the first stall.

"Hello?" His voice set off a series of responses from unseen horses. One kicked at the stall directly to his right, and he glanced toward the sound to find himself face to face with the white of a snorting, black stallion's eye. The orb rolled beneath the thick, black fringe of the animal's forelock. Recognizing a borderline crazed horse when confronted with one,

Adrien slowly extended his hand in peace.

The offer was rebuked with a powerful blast of air from the horse's flared nostrils.

Adrien lowered his hand and stepped back lest the jet-black beast's agitation provoked it to bite. With a toss of its enormous head and long, silky mane, the horse melded back into the shadows of the stall.

Aware of being watched, Adrien glanced toward the next stall to find another horse gazing curiously at him. The graceful lines of the head, the eye, the lustrous forelock, all a perfect match to its temperamental neighbor. Black stallions were far from rare, but to have two so perfectly matched? He moved closer and extended his hand, just as he'd done with the other beast. This stallion did not shy away. It pushed its muzzle against his palm and blew softly. The response sparked a memory.

Tattersalls. Three years ago. There had been a pair of matched blacks up for auction, their bloodlines so pure every gentlemen in London coveted them. He and Sam had been the last two bidders, the price having scared all the others away. In the end, he had conceded to Sam, who seemed intent to bankrupt the family coffers in order to possess the pair. It had been a friendly rivalry, mostly because Sam had walked away the victor.

When Adrien had gone to congratulate Sam, he'd had a chance to watch as the pair were loaded up for transport. Night and day, he had suggested Sam name them, given the differences in their temperament. One trotted into the conveyance calm as you please while the other tossed its head, yanked its lead free, and knocked two stable hands to the ground as it reared to paw the air. Adrien had stepped forward in an attempt to calm the beast, but Sam had been faster. A few good lashings and the beast had been cowed into obedience.

He looked at the docile stallion before him. Its eyes were closed in appreciation of the stroke of Adrien's hand. A veritable angel of a horse, despite its size and devilish appearance. Was it possible?

With a soft word of apology for cutting the petting short, he stepped back to the other stall. Its occupant continued to haunt the back wall, one foreleg pawing at the hay in obvious restlessness and unease. Frowning, he moved to the carriage. Without the aid of adequate light, it was difficult to make out details, but he could see the side panel was devoid of any crest. The lack put Adrien on high alert. After all, only a fool would kidnap a lady while using their own personal carriage, and Sam was no fool.

"Can I help ye?"

Adrien turned and was instantly blinded by the full, unfiltered blaze of a lantern. He held up a hand to shield his eyes. "Are you the stable master?"

"Aye, but you ain't the owner of that fine carriage so I suggest you be steppin' away nice and slow."

Holding his hands up, Adrien did as the man instructed. "My horse is just outside—"

"Aye, I saw the beast. Threw a shoe by the looks of him."

"Yes, exactly. I had hoped to rectify the problem then be on my way."

The man lowered his lantern, revealing a rough, scowling countenance beneath the brim of a crushed hat. "Can you pay?"

"Of course." Adrien dropped his hands. The man

did not appear to be armed, just cautious and a tad rude. "I'll pay you more than fair price for a shoe and the use of the tools, but I mean to do the deed myself."

"Good, because I ain't your lacky."

Well, then.

The man shuffled closer and shot a curse toward the stall to his right as the swinging light from the lantern enraged the temperamental stallion. "Damned demon wouldn't even let me rub him down, and now I got a bleedin' lord up my arse for not obeyin' his orders."

"Did you catch his name, by chance?"

"Eh?" The man squinted at Adrien. "Who? The horse?"

"No. The bleedin' lord."

"Aye, I think it was Penlay or Penlick or Petlick or some such. All them lords and their fancy names sound the same to me." He brushed by Adrien to hang the lantern on a wall hook.

"Petley?"

He shrugged. "Aye, maybe." While opening the tack room door, he glanced over his shoulder with a rather alarming smile. "Had a real fine lady with him though. Red hair, milky skin, a good set of—"

"Yes, quite. I assume they've taken a room at the inn?" It took every ounce of Adrien's willpower not to bolt from the stables and charge into the inn.

"What? Are you daft? Why the devil would his lordship leave his horseflesh here then hie off somewhere else? Of course they are in the bleedin' inn. Cor," the man scoffed, "are you drunk or stupid, mate?"

"In response to the former, unfortunately, no. As for the latter—"

"All that fancy talk makes me head hurt." The man ended the conversation by disappearing into the tack room. In moments, he emerged with a horseshoe in one hand and the necessary tools in the other. "Are you sure you know what you're doin', guv'nor? Most blokes who talk fancy can't lace their own drawers let alone shoe a horse."

"How right you are. I will double your fee if you see to the task and make my mount as comfortable as a king."

"Aye, aye. I ain't got nothin' against your fine mount, guv'nor. He'll be sighin' in pleasure in no time or my name ain't Johnny Dickin."

"Keep him away from that one," Adrien pointed to the first stall. "Chevalier has an excellent temperament, but he'll pick a fight if need be."

"Aye, aye, no need to worry, ol' Johnny knows what's what with horses. Go on then, guv'nor, it's clear as day you got business of some sort with the fancy lord who owns that there carriage. Never say I delayed you."

"You're a good man, Johnny Dickin." Adrien passed the man a gold coin. "Take good care of Chev, and there'll be more where that came from."

He left Johnny gnawing on the edge of the coin and made his way outside. After a brief moment to comfort a restless Chevalier, he headed for the inn.

He had to duck to enter the taproom and remain stooped to avoid scalping himself as he traversed the floor with its buckled, heaving planks. Reaching the back counter without incident, he rang the small, copper bell. A young maid emerged from behind a swinging door to toss him a scowl that would have put ol' Johnny Dickin's to shame.

"What you be needin' then?" She hovered far behind the counter, as if wanting to remain out of arm's reach of him. "A room? A meal?"

"Neither, I merely wish to inquire about a pair of guests—"

"Talk plain. I ain't got time for your fancy airs. This place don't run itself, don't you know?"

"Of course it does not. Forgive me." His words softened her expression, but not by much. "Johnny mentioned a lord and lady had checked in."

"Aye." She nodded. "So they did. What's it to you?" In a manner that seemed unselfconscious, the girl lifted a hand to rub at her cheek, drawing Adrien's attention to what looked to be a fresh bruise. "No," she went on before he could reply, "let me guess. Yer chasin' after the lady, ain't you? I could tell she weren't happy to be with his lordship, I could." Her watery, hooded gaze raked over him. "I'd have stabbed the gent with a hairpin to return to the likes you, I would."

"You are too kind."

She moved to the counter and leaned her weight upon her forearms. Doing so allowed her loose-fitting blouse to gape and expose her small, rose-tipped breasts. "No doubt you're here to take her back, eh? If she won't have you, though she'd be daft to say no, you know where to find me, you do."

"I am flattered, but in all honesty, I pray your company will not be required to ease the sting of rejection."

She straightened and shrugged her blouse back into place. "You'll be wantin' to know where to find them, is that right?"

"Your beauty is only outdone by your sharp wit."

"Cor, talk like that will have me crawling over this counter, it will. Mind that wicked tongue of yours." She blushed behind her bruising. "Room 6C. Up one flight and located at the end of the corridor at the top of another set of stairs. I figured Lord Uppity would be wantin' the best The Devil's Inn had to offer."

Adrien slid a coin across the counter. *"Merci beaucoup, mademoiselle."*

Her eyes widened as she snatched up the coin. "A Frog, are you?" She bit into the coin, then dropped it down her bodice. "Might be treasonous of me to say it, but my offer still stands if you find yourself needin' a bit of comfort."

"Not treasonous at all, I assure you." He left her with a wink and stalked toward the narrow staircase. He took the steps three at a time, then slowed his pace upon reaching the corridor. There was no telling what frame of mind Sam might be in, and barging in like a marauding pirate would do none of them any good, most especially Eirene.

That being said, Adrien wished he had brought a pistol. Knowing Sam as he did, the man would not yield peacefully.

Chapter Fifteen

Eirene stepped back from the edge of the bed and employed Petley's handkerchief to wipe the perspiration from her forehead. As it turned out, he had not died, though death might have been preferable to what he had endured over the last two hours or so. She glanced around the room, searching for a clock, but no such luck. She supposed he likely had a pocket watch tucked inside his waistcoat, but she hadn't the motivation to search the pile of clothing she had tossed over the foot of the bed. She hadn't the motivation to do much of anything. Seeing him through the throes of his illness had taxed her to her very core. The man had carried on like a child.

Part of her had wished to consign him to the devil, but she would not have been able to live with the guilt. Her grandfather would have shaken his head in disappointment, saying something to the effect of, "*One cannot escape one's enemy if unwilling to destroy.*"

"Yes, well," she said to the room, "sorry, Grandpapa, but I'll not have this fiend's blood on my hands, no matter his intentions toward me." Though if Petley truly meant to do away with her once in possession of her fortune, she might have to revisit her opinion of his death. Self-defense was vastly different from murder, after all.

The scrape of footsteps from the outer corridor

drew her gaze toward the door. Likely the maid had come to clear the plates. As she moved toward the door she wondered if she should mention the bad food. Assuming the maid did not know. There was always the off chance the girl had been fully aware of the poor quality and simply did not care. After all, Petley had struck the girl with alarming force. Perhaps the bad food was meant as retaliation?

Eirene pulled open the door, but it was not the maid who stood on the other side. "Adrien?"

She blinked, but he did not vanish. He stood there as real as could be, dressed in riding clothes and several layers of road dust. His ashen complexion, gaunt cheeks, and dull gaze did nothing to improve his appearance, yet she'd never laid eyes upon a sight more welcoming.

He had come for her. Adrien, looking as though he had escaped his own funeral, had come for her.

She had never fancied herself a female to be moved by such a display of masculine possession, and yet, she was. Very moved. Almost to tears, damn the man and his ability to muddle her emotions.

His gaze took in every inch of her. "Are you hurt? Did he touch you? Where the devil is the bastard?"

He shoved past her to enter the room and drew to an abrupt halt as he caught sight of Petley sprawled, naked, upon the bed. The thin, worn, oft repaired sheet offered little modesty.

Adrien whipped around to face her, his eyes no longer dull. "I see."

"No, you do not see, at all." How dare he stand there and jump to such an offensive conclusion. Yes, Petley was naked in the bed, but was she? No. She slammed the door and crossed her arms. "Do not look at me like that, sir. *That*"—she gestured toward the bed—"is most definitely *not* what it appears to be."

"No?" He too crossed his arms. "So it is not Lord Samuel Petley naked in bed?"

"Of course it is, but he is not in his current state for the reasons your corrupt mind has invented." Had she really expected Adrien to sweep her into his arms and profess how relieved he was to find her well? How foolish. No wonder she had never allowed herself to become enamored of fairy tales.

"No?" He shot a venomous look toward the bed. "The man looks as if he's been ridden near to death." His stare returned to her. "And I must say, you look a tad feverish as well."

She fisted her hands at her sides. "If I were not so damned relieved to see you, I would blacken both your eyes." Her threat drew her attention to the darkness that marred the left side of his jaw. Her ire eased as she recalled Petley's boast about attacking Adrien and reached out to brush her fingers along the bruise. "It is not as bad as his words led me to fear."

Adrien clasped her wrist, not to remove her touch but to prolong it. "Outwardly, no, but my ribs tell a much different tale. Riding hell for leather after you did them no favors, I might add."

"I'll not apologize for that which is in no way my fault."

"No, you will not." He used his hold on her wrist to tug her forward. When her body collided with his, he flinched and sucked in a sharp breath but would not allow her to break the embrace. "No. No. Let me hold you. Please." He wrapped his arms around her and tucked her tight to his chest. Propping his chin atop her head, he sighed into her hair. "I was terrified I would be too late."

Eirene said nothing. She simply absorbed the feel of being in Adrien's arms. Odd to think she had decided to live without this, whatever *this* was. It felt like the nonsense her mother used to wax poetic about. Before her father had turned into a drunken cheat and broken the woman's heart. Her mother had called it love. She had told Eirene, time after time, she would recognize it when it happened.

There's no ignoring it, my darling. Mark my words. You'll feel equal parts sick and giddy. You'll believe you've lost all reason, but it'll be your heart you've lost.

It sounds dreadful, she'd told her mother.

Her mother had laughed at that. *It is only dreadful if it ends, my darling.*

A prophetic statement, though neither of them had known at the time that her father would cease loving her mother in order to bestow his affections upon cards, drink, and loose women. When the combination had finally killed him, her mother had become a different woman. Gone was the dewy-eyed, lovestruck bride. In her place was a cynical, shattered shell who begged her fourteen-year-old daughter never to fall in love. Never to allow a man to destroy her. Never to surrender her heart.

Less than a year later, her mother had died in her sleep, an empty bottle of laudanum upended on the pillow beside her.

The unpleasant chill of moisture upon her cheek brought Eirene crashing back to the present. She pulled free of Adrien's embrace and turned her back so he would not see her tears. But she had not been fast enough.

"Eirene?" His hands landed upon her shoulders, and he turned her back around. "Anything but tears, *ma couer*, I beg you."

His heart. God help her, he had referred to her as his heart. Did he believe himself in love with her? Yes, he had proposed, but she hadn't believed the offer to come from a place motivated by love, for heaven's sake. Affection? Perhaps. Attraction? Most certainly. But love?

A tortured groan sounded from the bed, drawing her attention and Adrien's as well. Petley kicked about under the light weight of the sheet, dislodging the covering in a most inappropriate fashion. She did not bother to avert her gaze. She'd been the one to strip the man of his clothes, after all, and after witnessing the repeated emptying of his bowels and gut, nothing about his body could possibly shock her.

"You claim this is not what it looks like," Adrien remarked with his gaze locked upon Petley. "What, exactly, is it then?"

****

Adrien stared at Eirene, waiting for her response but wanting nothing more than to drag her from the room, toss her onto Chevalier and hurry her back to London. Why the hell he did not was a mystery he seemed too fatigued to sort.

She sighed, dislodging a coil of hair that lay plastered to her moist cheek. "The idiot consumed a bad meat pie." Crossing her arms, she looked at him and shrugged. "At first I thought he'd been poisoned, and I imagined all sorts of horrific scenarios, all ending with me dangling from a noose."

"Jesu."

"Quite." Her gaze fell upon the bed. "I had to do something about his screams, lest they wake the dead, or worse, the local magistrate."

"Assuming this God forsaken place has a magistrate." Adrien's comment earned him a brief smile before she continued to explain how Petley had come to be naked in bed.

"Carried on like a man having a limb amputated, screaming about being on fire, about wanting to die." She looked to Adrien. "At one point, he begged me to let him die. How's that for being tested, hmm? As tempted as I was, I had no desire to have his blood on my hands, so I smacked him a few times across the face to settle his hysteria and asked what I could do to relieve some of his discomfort. I barely had time to remove his clothing before the meat decided it had spent enough time *inside* his body." She arched a brow at Adrien lest he mistake her meaning. "What followed does not need to be revisited. Suffice to say, his lordship will survive to inflict more of his offensive arrogance upon the world."

"How is it that you were not similarly afflicted?" He had noticed the two empty plates upon the small table beneath the window.

"I have an aversion to eating anything that smells like a horse's arse. Petley obviously does not possess such standards."

"So it would seem." Moving to the side of the bed, Adrien picked up Petley's discarded coat and dropped it across the man's poorly concealed groin. "Forgive me for assuming—"

"That I would fornicate with that man?"

The sharpness of her tone brought him around to face her. The expression she wore was no softer.

"Hamish suspected Petley meant to take you to Gretna?"

"Yes, and once we were legally wed and he in control of my vast fortune, I imagine I would have found myself locked in the attic, buried in an unmarked grave, or committed to Bedlam." She frowned. "What would provoke a man of Petley's standing to go to such extremes? I understand he might require money to pay off debts, but surely he could have courted and married any number of the young heiresses running about London. Why me?"

"If I had to guess, I'd say it was your status as a recluse that moved you to the top of the list. After all, who would miss a recluse?" Adrien saw Eirene visibly shiver, but he did not go to her. As much as he longed to soothe the sting of his words, he did nothing. She had turned away from his embrace in an attempt to hide her tears. If ever there was a woman disinclined to accept the comfort of a man, it was Eirene. Forcing such affection would get him nowhere.

And doing nothing would gain him what?

He shook his head and cursed Fate for allowing him to fall in love with such a prickly, complicated, amazing woman.

"I do not believe we should be here when Petley comes around," she said, breaking into his musings. "His mood is bound to be as sour as his digestion."

"Of course, *oui*." He raked a hand through his hair and frowned at the palm of his riding glove, which now bore a thin layer of dust. *Mon Dieu*, he had to look a fright. "Chevalier threw a shoe—"

"We will borrow his lordship's carriage. His team has had ample time to rest." She nodded once, as if he had voiced approval of the idea, then made quick work of shrugging into her spencer and cramming a few pins into her tangled hair.

"Eirene."

She glanced over her shoulder and arched a brow in lieu of speaking, and he saw the pins wedged between her lush lips. "Hmm?"

"When we return to London, what are your plans?"

She spit the pins into her hand. "I will collect Hamish and leave for the country. This time, I shall refrain from taking a walk, though I never would have imagined his lordship so bold as to snatch a lady from the street in broad daylight." She scowled toward the bed. "I have learned a great lesson about underestimating one's enemy."

"I do not want you to leave London." He halved the distance between them and halted as she began to back away. "Eirene, please, hear me out."

"No." She shook her head with enough force to dislodge some of the recently placed pins. They fell to floor unremarked. "We are not having this conversation. Not here. Not in London. Not ever."

"You have no idea what I intend to say."

"No?" She threw up her hands, then let them fall to her sides as if they were made of stone. "I believe I know exactly what you mean to say, Adrien, and it will prove nothing. I have no desire to wed, not you, not any man. My opinion of the matter will not change, so I am begging you to say no more on the subject or I will be forced to forgo the pleasure of your company on my return trip to London."

"The pleasure of my company?" How dare she use such words after throwing his affections for her in his face? He was beginning to wonder if Lady Rowe-Weston possessed a heart or if it had been lost amidst the militant lessons of her grandfather. If ever there was a man Adrien wished he could challenge to a duel, it was the late earl. What right did the man have for treating his granddaughter like a soldier? For raising her to be cold and calculating? To leave her all alone, believing herself unworthy of being loved?

Anger fueled his next words. "If it's the pleasure of my company you crave, never let it be said, I left a lady disappointed."

Chapter Sixteen

Eirene backed away as Adrien advanced. His pewter eyes flashed with anger. She threw up her hands. "You would not dare force yourself upon me."

He halted, as if he'd reached the end of an invisible tether. "Force myself upon you? *Mere de Dieu.*" He raked a dusty glove through his hair and cursed and peeled off both gloves before throwing them across the room in an impressive display of temper. "Is that what you truly believe my intentions are in this moment? No." He held up a hand to silence her before she could reply. "Allow me to hazard a guess, hmm? Was it your grandfather who informed you that a man must never be trusted when in the grips of his passion? Or perhaps your mother? Did she teach you that a man will always take what he wants from y—"

"Stop." She did not yell. Nor did she need to. He snapped his mouth shut like a hound closing its jaws around a fresh kill. "No, I do not believe you intend to take me by force. Of course, I do not believe that."

"Then, please, explain why you said what you said."

She threw her hands up in helpless surrender. "I do not know. Damn it all to hell. I. Do. Not. Know."

A soldier must never show weakness in the face of the enemy—

Oh, do shut up, Grandfather!

"Eirene." Adrien stood before her, her hands clasped in his, his pewter eyes no longer flashing with anger. "Talk to me."

Talk to him? Talk to him? What did he want her to say, precisely? That he confused her? That he had disrupted her well-structured universe with a mere glimpse of his bloody collarbone? Ha! Talk to him, indeed. She was tired of talking. Tired of calculating every word before it fell from her tongue. Tired of... Well, she was simply tired. She'd been kidnapped, dragged across country, forced to prevent a scoundrel from choking to death on his own vomit, and that was not even the worst of it.

Oh no. The worst, the *absolute* worst, was coming to the realization that she was in *love*. She, Lady Eirene Rowe-Weston, a cold-hearted, reclusive woman of great wealth, who had vowed to live out her days in a state of euphoric independence with not a gentleman caller in sight, was in love. And with a rogue, no less. A French rogue. A French rogue masquerading as a French noble. Dear God. How was any of this happening to *her*?

"Eirene? I cannot read your thoughts, but your expression is rather terrifying."

"Adrien, I..." She shook her head, unsure how to proceed. Perhaps a list would help. If only Adrien didn't have a hold of her hands.

He tightened said hold and pulled her toward him. "Adrien, what? I wish to return to London? Regret my poorly constructed plan for ruination? Wish I had allowed Petley to die? Want you madly? Love you?" He flashed a boyish, crooked smile that pierced her heart like a sharpened hat pin while toppling what might remain of her well-constructed universe.

"Adrien, I want you to kiss me."

He blinked. Then again. *"Pardonez moi?"*

"I believe you not only heard me but understood perfectly."

"Oh yes, I heard you and understood you."

"Well? What are you waiting for then?"

He smiled. The cad smiled. "You did not say please."

"Oh, for heaven's sake." Like her grandfather always said, if you want something done correctly, simply do it yourself.

Eirene lurched toward Adrien and slammed her mouth into his. The move lacked any semblance of grace or finesse, but it achieved the goal. That of their lips pressed together. She relied on his instincts as a rogue to take over—ah, yes. He released her hands in order to wrap his arms around her and pull her tight to his body. He angled his lips just so. The kiss changed. Softened? No. There was nothing *soft* about the pressure of his lips against hers or the insertion of his tongue into her mouth.

One of his hands gripped her nape, angling her head back just a tad. His tongue delved deeper. God help her…

She clung to his shoulders and attempted to find a way to rationalize how a kiss could make her feel as though the blood in her veins had turned to molten lava. But as his tongue stroked alongside hers and as his teeth nibbled oh-so-gently at the fullness of her upper lip, she realized one crucial fact. There was no rationalizing the way she felt while in his arms. Passion could not be dissected or analyzed in any way that might make it easier to understand. It was simply there. To be experienced.

"I do believe I can actually taste the depth of your thoughts, Eirene." He spoke against her lips, between nibbles. "Care to share what has the power to distract you from my kissing expertise?"

She separated her mouth from his. Really? Did he actually expect her to formulate coherent sentences while their lips were pressed together? "I was contemplating passion."

His eyes widened. "Oh? And? What has that analytical brain of yours deduced?"

"That it cannot be analyzed."

"I see." He stepped back to hold her at arm's length. His gaze swept her head to toe, then fixed once more upon her eyes. "You are wrong." He shook his head as she parted her lips to speak. "*Oui*, passion as an emotion cannot be weighed and measured, no more than love or hate or fear, but the effects of passion can be studied."

"The effects? Do you refer to—" Before she could finish the question, he had her hand pressed to the front of his trousers. "Oh…" She flexed her fingers around his arousal, marveling at the thought that, although he had been wedged between her legs and pressed against her sex, the *feel* of him in her hand seemed so much more intimate. Especially when he pulsed against her palm.

She tightened her grip in an effort to have the tantalizing phenomena repeated.

"Are you attempting to make me go off?"

Her gaze snapped to his. "Excuse me?"

"Continue to squeeze the trigger and the gun will

fire. Surely, your grandfather taught you that simple lesson?" He encircled her wrist with his fingers when she attempted to snatch her hand back. "Oh, no, no, no. I like it. Your hand on me."

Her cheeks flared hot. Lord. Had she ever blushed in her entire life as much as she had in the brief time spent in this man's company?

She met his pewter gaze. "What do we do now?"

His smile was patient. "I am but your humble servant, my lady. I will do whatever you ask of me."

She worried her bottom lip between her teeth. "If I were to order you to return me to my country estate and forget about me, you would?"

"No." He did not even hesitate for half a heartbeat.

Eirene managed to wiggle her hand free of his. She could not continue this conversation while gripping his…well! "You claimed you were mine to command, and yet, you say no."

"Permit me to clarify, my lady. *Oui*, I will see to your safe arrival in the country. No, I will not forget about you. For as long as I live." He did not touch her. He made no move to touch her. He merely held her gaze with a sincerity that clawed at her heart.

"I see." She crossed her arms and turned to the window. She needed to escape that pewter gaze. It saw too much. Had always seen too much, from the moment they had first made eye contact in her grandfather's study.

"Marry me, Eirene."

She closed her eyes. "Adrien—"

His hands clasped her shoulders, but he did not turn her to face him. "Your turmoil is a palpable presence in this room, and do you know why you are in such turmoil? Hmm?" He went on before she could think to reply. "It is because you are at war, and it is not a war your grandfather prepared you to fight."

He finally turned her to face him, and she prayed he could not detect the moisture in her eyes. "Adrien, I am not engaged in any sort of war. I do not wish to marry. Period. Why must you belabor the issue?"

"Because you cannot see what I see when you speak those words."

"Oh? Do tell."

He released one of her shoulders in order to slip a finger beneath her chin to angle her face upward. "Repeat after me. Adrien, I have no wish to marry you."

She did not fully see the usefulness of the exercise, but nevertheless, she humored him by repeating the phrase in what she believed to be a steady, non-affected tone.

"When you lie, your left eye twitches ever so slightly."

She pulled free of his grasp. "This is ridiculous."

Damn the infuriating man to hell. Her grandfather had warned her many times of just that particular weakness. He had told her, time after time, nothing gives the enemy the advantage faster than a foolish tell. She had believed herself cured of the habit and capable of lying with great aplomb if need be.

"I possess no such tell, Monsieur Cloutier."

"That is a lie."

She ground her back teeth together. "Will you or will you not escort me back to the country?"

"I said I would, and I am not a man to go back upon my word. Much to Cyril's disgust."

Petley chose that moment to expound a great trembling moan of shocking volume.

Eirene nearly jumped out of her skin, but Adrien merely tossed a glance toward the bed.

"What are we to do with him?" she asked.

"Toss him out the window?"

She could not help but smile at his enthusiastic suggestion. "Tempting, but I believe you will have more than enough to deal with, come morning, without adding murder."

Adrien frowned. "Petley informed you of his plan to ruin me?"

"He did, and with great pride."

Petley moaned again, then suddenly sat up and looked around in abject horror. "Where the devil am I? What the devil happened? Where the devil are my bloody clothes?" His gaze found Adrien. "What the devil are *you* doing here?"

****

Adrien ignored Petley's scathing question. "You should be on your knees thanking Lady Rowe-Weston for not allowing you to die."

Petley's attention shifted beyond Adrien's shoulder to rest, no doubt, upon Eirene. "Thank her? The bitch attempted to poison me. I'll see her hung, I will. Mark my—"

"I see I should have let you die," Eirene calmly interjected.

Adrien sidestepped to block Petley's view of her. "Everyone in this room knows Lady Rowe-Weston made no attempt to poison you, Petley. Now shut your mouth and listen to the way things are going to be."

Petley's dark eyes narrowed to slits. "How dare

you speak to me in such a fashion, *peasant*." With a level of dignity that could only be mustered by one born to be noble, he gathered the worn sheet about him and climbed to his feet. The man smelled like an old chamber pot, looked like a freshly unearthed corpse, and swayed like a drunken sailor, but damn if he didn't glare down his nose at Adrien like the umpteenth generation English lord that he was.

"Come morning," Petley snarled, "all of London will know of your deception. There will be no one for you to turn to, not even my kind-hearted cousin is stupid enough to offer shelter or friendship to a fraud. You will be an outcast. An exile. The shame will—"

"I know Jillian is your daughter."

Sam blinked then collapsed onto the bed like he'd been shot in the chest. The arrogance leeched out of his gaze faster than blood from a stuck pig. "She is an innocent."

"*Oui*, and that is why you will do exactly as I say."

****

"Do you believe Petley will do as you instructed?" Eirene asked the question while staring out the carriage window. The lights of London had just come into view after a very long, very quiet trip from the inn. She had decided against traveling to her country estate, for two reasons. One, she had no wish to prolong Adrien's obvious physical agony. And two, she had no wish to prolong her own emotional agony, which intensified with each moment she spent in his company. Once away from him, she would be able to think and rationalize. She would make a list to prove her rejection of his proposal made perfect sense. Perhaps she would send him the list.

"I believe he will wish to keep Jillian's reputation as untarnished as possible. Besides," Adrien said while attempting to shift his body on the bench. Each movement caused a gasp of pain, which in turn, caused a most singular sensation in the vicinity of her heart. "Sam is an intelligent, charming scoundrel. I have no doubt he will remake his fortune in America and Jillian will be a belle of Society."

"I shall say a prayer each night for the American heiresses."

"Indeed." On that note, Adrien put his head back and closed his eyes.

Eirene assumed he meant to rest a while longer. One should never assume, her grandfather would always warn. And Adrien proved him right.

"We did not finish our conversation, Eirene."

"Oh?" She twisted her hands together in her lap. "And what conver—"

"Don't." Adrien lifted his head and met her gaze. "Please. Don't prevaricate. I lack the patience to play games."

"Very well. You speak of our conversation regarding the future you wish us to have."

"*Oui.*"

"It is not a future I wish us to have." It took every ounce of control she possessed to prevent her left eye from twitching. "There. Conversation concluded."

The carriage drew to a halt before her townhome, and a heavy, awkward and rather painful silence fell between them. She reached for the door, but his hand covered hers.

"Look at me," he ordered.

"I would rather—"

"Look at me, damn you."

She schooled her features, or so she prayed, then did as he commanded.

His fingers tightened atop hers. "Say it again."

"What, exactly, is it you wish me to repeat?"

"Tell me there is no place for me in your future."

Eirene's heart raced, and the blood heated in her veins. She felt rather ill, of a sudden. "There is no future for us."

Adrien released her hand and settled back against the squabs. "Go." He closed his eyes. *"Aller. S'il vous plait."*

She jumped as the door was wrenched from her light grasp. The coachman offered a hand. She hesitated, more confused in that moment than she had ever been in her entire lifetime. She gazed at Adrien, silently begging him to look at her. But he did not. He kept his head back and his eyes closed.

"My lady?"

She managed a grateful smile for the coachman as she took his hand and stepped down. The door of her home opened to reveal Hamish, visibly shaking with relief. He rushed toward her, breaking every protocol possible between mistress and servant. She stood her ground, aware of a series of little sounds. The coachman mumbling a "Good day." The carriage door closing. The carriage springs squeaking. The horses shifting.

"My lady, I am beside myself with relief." Hamish took both her hands in his, then glanced past her as the carriage rolled away. "And the vicomte? Is he well?"

"I would very much like to rest, Hamish." She freed her hands, gathered her skirts, and entered the house without allowing the urge to stare after the carriage to get the better of her. Her grandfather had always said, there is nothing to be gained by looking back.

Chapter Seventeen

Adrien sat before the dying fire and slouched deep in his chair with his booted feet upon the fender. A third glass of fine, French cognac rested upon his thigh, the first two having left behind a low buzzing in his head. Cyril, after finally giving up all attempts to convince Adrien to accompany him, had gone out for the night. Sayers had appeared at Adrien's elbow some time ago to say the servants had gone to bed and to inquire as to whether *his lordship* required anything. Adrien had replied with a brusque shake of his head while wondering what Sayers' reaction would be if the butler were to discover he waited upon his equal.

After returning from his mad dash to rescue Eirene and, of course, explaining what had transpired, Adrien had insisted Cyril tell the servants the truth before they read it in the morning paper. Cyril had refused, saying if he wished the servants to know, he could damn well tell them himself.

He had said nothing, choosing to hold onto the hope that perhaps Sam had been lying when threatening to expose him.

But Sam had not been lying. The paper Adrien had barely glanced at, some five hours ago upon waking late, had declared quite boldly that Vicomte Benoit was a fraud.

Staring into the fire, he sipped his drink, but the

flavor he had appreciated only moments before was now as palatable as dust upon his tongue. He could not help but speculate how his friends had reacted to the truth. Kilby, a man with his own secrets, perhaps would understand and sympathize, assuming anyone allowed Adrien a chance to explain the deception. Westhaven, too, had secrets, and Venton... Well, only God knew the full details of that demon's past. Ha! Perhaps the four of them could form their own exclusive club, a safe haven for any rake with a ruinous skeleton hiding in their wardrobe.

Adrien laughed around his next sip, realizing Petley would make a fine member as well. Oh, the irony. Hell, every rake in London likely had a damning secret. After all, not everyone could be as upstanding as Cyril.

The sound of the door opening nearly caused Adrien to groan out loud. He did not check to see who it was, but it could only be Sayers, as he'd not heard Cyril return. "What is it, Sayers? Have you come to toss my no good, common body into the streets before your master returns?"

He took another long swallow of cognac, wishing it would numb the pain in his chest and erase the scene that played over and over in his head. That of Eirene stepping down from Petley's carriage and walking into her home without so much as a glance over her shoulder. No doubt, by now, she was safely ensconced within her precious country estate. Did she even think of him? Surely, she would have seen the morning paper. Had she read the article and breathed a sigh of relief to be well rid of him?

The door closed with a decisive click, followed by

the sound of light footsteps moving across the room. His fingers tightened on the glass, and his alcohol riddled senses attempted to focus. There was no way the footsteps belonged to Sayers, and none of the maids had cause to be in the room until dawn.

Eliminating Sayers and the rest of the servants as owners of the footsteps left Adrien feeling more than a tad vulnerable, and he eased himself forward in the chair to curl his hand around one of the fire pokers. Sam might be on his way to America, but he was also a man who did not tolerate being bested. Adrien would not be surprised if Petley had arranged an assassination attempt before departing.

After all, his last words to Adrien, before being left behind at the inn, had been, "I suggest you adopt the habit of sleeping with one eye open, *peasant*. As for your whore—"

Adrien's fist had knocked Sam out cold before he could finish his little speech.

The footsteps stopped, refocusing Adrien's full attention to the present matter, that of an unknown intruder. He remained as he was, bent forward, cognac in one hand, makeshift weapon in the other. His head buzzed with cognac, and he cursed the quantity he'd consumed.

"Had I imagined you would arm yourself against me, I would have brought my pistol."

In an ungainly mess of spilled drink and clattering iron, Adrien lurched to his feet and swung around to meet Eirene's gaze over the back of the wing chair. How? Why? What the actual hell was she doing here?

Before he could find his tongue, she flashed a smile, albeit a cautious one, and continued her journey across the room. The pain in his chest that he'd been attempting to numb intensified as he stared at her. Had she grown more beautiful? Were her freckles darker? More plentiful, perhaps? Hard to tell the farther she moved away from the one lamp Sayers had insisted upon lighting so as "not to leave your lordship wallowing in the dark."

She halted behind the chair and laid a hand upon the curved top. He stared at her bare fingers with their rounded nails and recalled the tentative way they had stroked his collarbone. *Mon Dieu*, it felt like a lifetime since she had touched him. Had it truly only been a mere twenty-four hours or so?

"Hello, Adrien." Hearing his name upon her lips was sweeter than anything he could pour into a glass.

"What the hell are you doing here?" His harsh words made her flinch, but he was too awash in cognac to temper his shock. He had thought never to see her again, yet here she stood, wearing the burgundy gown from their first meeting. *Sans* fichu. Perhaps he was hallucinating?

"By, here, do you refer to London or—"

"My room, Eirene. What the hell are you doing in my room?" He was afraid to move, afraid to blink, lest she vanish. "I believed you to be well away from the unpleasantness of London, yet here you are. Why?"

She lowered her gaze and idly caressed the curved back of the wing chair. If she meant to drive him mad, the sight of her fingers petting the damn chair was a good start. "If you must know the truth," she began while looking up at him once more, "I was halfway to the country and instructed the coachman to turn around."

Adrien's breath burned in his lungs. "Why?"

She licked her lips and visibly swallowed, but she did not break eye contact. "I did not want you to be alone when the news of your identity became public."

"Then you have wasted your time. The news is hours old, and as you can see—" He spread his arms to give her a good look at his disheveled person, open collar, wrinkled linen, mussed hair. "—I am none the worse for wear."

Sarcasm dripped from his tone, causing her to flinch again. *Mon Dieu*, why was he acting like such an ass?

"You are angry with me." She did not state it as a question, nor did he offer a reply. "Very well." She nodded once, in a most precise, definitive fashion.

It bothered Adrien to watch Eirene suffer his attitude, yet he did nothing to ease her agitation. He *was* angry with her. For a number of reasons. The least of which was how she had walked away without looking back, and he did not give a damn if that made him petty or childish.

"Would you like me to leave?" she asked while staring into his eyes.

Damn her. No, he did not want her to leave. He wanted her in his arms. In his bed.

The silence lengthened and thickened.

Eirene cleared her throat. "Very well. I see it was a mis—"

Adrien circled the chair as quick as any hound after a fox. Eirene gasped as he took her in his arms and captured her parted lips beneath his mouth.

"No." He kissed her. "I do not—" He kissed her again. "—want you to leave." Another kiss, long and deep this time. She clung to the front of his shirt, her breaths short and quick, exactly like a fox run to ground and cornered.

Adrien ended the kiss with a shake of his head. He really needed to cease with the bad analogies. Now was neither the time nor the place for such poetic nonsense.

"Adrien?" She spoke just above a hush, the sound like a seductive swipe of her tongue against his ear.

Mon Dieu, the woman had a way of addling his brain. Soon, he would be on one knee spouting the romantic drivel of Lord Byron. A display sure to leave the militant Lady Rowe-Weston unmoved.

Adrien looked into Eirene's amber eyes. "Tell me the real reason you came back."

"I told you. I did not wish for you to be alone—"

"You are lying." He ran his thumb along the delicate skin below her left eye as the muscle twitched. "Be honest with me, Eirene. I beg you."

****

Eirene disengaged herself from Adrien's embrace and took several steps back. He wanted honesty, did he? Where should she begin? Would he like to hear about the near collapse she had suffered upon entering her home and hearing the carriage drive away? Would he wish to know how panicked Hamish had become upon seeing his lady trembling from head to toe while tears streamed down her face? Would such lurid details make him happy?

Or perhaps she should share the moment leading to her decision to order the carriage turned about. Could she put into words the pain she had felt in her chest? The shortness of breath or the frantic tone of her voice as she banged on the carriage ceiling to demand the driver turn around with all due haste.

Or maybe he would like to know about a more recent moment. The moment when she had hesitated upon his front stoop, hand poised over the knocker, stomach in knots, heart in throat, fear causing her palms to perspire within her gloves. Should she detail for him the battle that had ensued between heart and brain? Her brain had demanded a list to outline the reasons she should knock versus the reasons she should not. Her heart had demanded she tell her brain to go to hell.

"Eirene?" Adrien somehow had a hold of her shoulders. When had he closed the distance between them? "You will give yourself wrinkles if you continue to think so deeply. Was my question really so difficult?"

She lifted her gaze to his. "I returned because I love you."

He smiled, and it was the most beautiful sight she'd ever witnessed. Then he did the most extraordinary thing. He swept her into his arms, like a gallant knight of yore, and carried her to the large, luscious looking bed where he laid her down with a gentleness that brought tears to her eyes.

She reached for him as he straightened, but he shook his head. "No, no. Allow me this moment to simply look at you." And look he did. His gaze trekked up and down her body with the diligence of a reconnaissance scout.

"I have a confession," he said as his eyes met hers. "I imagined how you would look in my bed that first day in your study."

Eirene pushed up to rest her weight upon her elbows. "And? Does reality meet with your expectations?"

"No." He offered nothing further as he began to unbutton his shirt.

She wanted to challenge his negative reply, but the sight of him shedding his clothing quite distracted her. He possessed a glorious physique, although the hard expanse of his torso was currently marred by ugly bruising.

She snapped her gaze to his face. "We cannot do this. You are in no condition."

He pushed his trousers down while shaking his head. "No, no. None of that. It is only bruising. I am fine." As if to prove his point, he lifted his arms over his head and did a number of fascinating twists and stretches. Eirene was quite certain the sight would fuel her dreams for years to come. "See? Hale and hearty as ever."

He was lying of course. She had noticed the subtle twinge of pain that crossed his features as he twisted his body to the left, but she said nothing. Male pride was a feisty beast if provoked, and the truth was, she wanted him to make love to her and she wanted it now.

She held out a hand. "Make love to me, Adrien."

"Avec plaisir, ma cherie."

Chapter Eighteen

Eirene did not need to ask twice.

Adrien crawled onto the bed over her supine body. Braced on hands and knees, he kissed her slightly parted lips, all while looking into her wide open eyes.

"Close your eyes, Eirene," he instructed around a smile and another kiss.

She shook her head. "I enjoy looking in your eyes when you kiss me."

He pulled back just enough to allow her to see his smile. She loved his smile, the way it made the corners of his eyes crinkle. It lent him a boyish vulnerability she doubted many people ever bore witness to. The papers would not write of him as they did if such a smile was commonplace. No, this smile was for her. Only for her. The realization should have thrilled, but it saddened her. She did not deserve to be the recipient of such a rare gift. She could not be what Adrien wanted her to be. He wanted a wife, maybe even a mother to his children. She could not be those things. Could she?

His kiss blessedly ended her train of thought. She focused on the feel of his lips, his warm breath, the moist slide of his tongue, his taste. Cognac. Well, well, well.

She eased away before he could kiss her again. "Have I fallen in love with a smuggler?"

His eyes narrowed in confusion.

"Your taste," she explained. "You taste like very fine cognac and, given the current situation with France…"

"Not only do you look like a fox, you are as keen as one." He landed a kiss upon her nose. "Westhaven is the smuggler."

"Westhaven?" She tried to imagine the charming man she'd met upon Lady Palmer's terrace as a smuggler. "I never would have guessed."

"And that is what makes him a very successful smuggler." He resumed kissing her, but she pulled away again, her mind working like a well-oiled mill.

"Westhaven. As in the son of Baron Eugene Westhaven of Cornwall?" If she were not mistaken, Baron Westhaven was the son of Navy Captain Edward Westhaven, an acquaintance of her grandfather's. He had passed a few years before her grandfather.

"Yes, Eirene, Henry hails from the Cornish Westhavens." Adrien sat back upon his heels, presenting a rather fetching image that made her forget all about the Westhavens. The man possessed sinfully glorious thighs, in or out of trousers.

She sat up so she could place her hands atop said thighs. The muscles tensed as Adrien sucked in a sharp breath. Other parts of him reacted in a most fascinating manner as well, and she gave into boldness and wrapped her right hand around his shaft.

"*Mon Dieu*, Eirene, have mercy."

She looked in Adrien's eyes. "Why? You do intend to make love to me, *oui*?" She worked her hand toward the tip, mesmerized by the sheen of moisture that appeared in response to the action.

Adrien captured her hand. "Yes, I intend to make

love to you. Make love, being the important phrase, but if you continue to torment me in such a fashion, I will send my intentions to hell, flip up your skirts, and ravish you like a rutting beast."

"Hmm." She slicked her hand back down his shaft, the movement aided by the liquid he'd expelled. "I like the sound of that." She barely had a chance to catch Adrien's gaze before he shoved her onto her back and took hold of her skirts.

"Tu es un vilain petit renard."

Eirene attempted to translate the murmured French, but it was difficult to think with his lips fused over hers, especially while his hands did truly wicked things beneath her skirts. When his fingers brushed over her sex, she gasped, but the slight touch was a poor warning for what followed.

Lord help her.

She arched her back and dropped her legs open like a wanton as he slipped a finger inside her. "Oh…"

"Do you like that, *ma cherie*?" His mouth was at her ear, his breath hot in her hair. "Hmm?" He pushed his finger deeper, and she purred like a cat. "*Oui*, I thought so," he said, with all the arrogant confidence of a born rogue. But he was *her* rogue.

"Adrien," she panted as he worked his finger in and out of her slick passage.

"Tell me what you want."

She grasped his shoulders. "You."

Almost before the word faded to silence, his hands were under her bottom, lifting her to accept the thrust of his erection. "*Mon Dieu*, you deserve better than this."

But he did not temper his movements. He filled her and withdrew, only to fill her again. It was breathtaking and primal and the most amazing sensation one could imagine.

She dug her nails into his shoulders. "Give me all you believe I deserve later, but for now…" She had to pause to catch her breath as he thrust forward again. "I beg you, do not stop."

"Never," he vowed while catching her lips for a deep, open-mouthed kiss.

****

Adrien smiled at nothing in particular as Eirene nestled against his side. Her naked body radiated heat and her hair smelled like wildflowers. *La vie était bonne.* Life was good.

"Thank you." Her quiet words broke the silence.

His smile widened as he kissed the top of her head. "It was my pleasure."

And it had been. Every second of it. Being inside Eirene, hearing his name on her lips, witnessing her awakening as she climaxed for the first time—all of it, a divine, life-changing pleasure.

"It would seem," she murmured while shifting at his side. "I am now, officially, ruined." Her movements indicated she had cocked her head to look at him in the dark. "Should we hang the bed sheet from the window to declare my fallen woman status to the masses?"

Adrien's blood ran cold. "You did not bleed."

She sat up at that, and he could feel the weight of her regard. "I did not?"

"No." Adrien remained as he was, staring at the ceiling. "It is not uncommon, especially for a woman who enjoys riding astride."

"And how would you know how I enjoy riding?"

"A man can tell." Now he sat up as well, cursing

the lack of light within the partially enclosed bed. "You rode me with breathtaking skill." The words fell between them, sounding as dead as he suddenly felt.

"Should I consider that a compliment?" The laugh that followed sounded hollow.

He focused on the shadowy outline of her form. Maybe it was best to have this conversation in the dark. "You have no intention of becoming my wife, do you?"

He did not require an answer. He knew. He'd known the moment she made the flippant comment about the bed sheet. But he wanted an answer. He wanted to hear her reject her feelings for him.

"Adrien, making love with you did not alter my view of marriage. Why would you believe it would?"

"Because obviously I'm a bloody fool." He left the bed, needing to be away from her and her damn narrow view of things. He stalked across the room to pour a drink. The bed springs creaked, followed by the soft pad of bare feet. He gripped the glass tighter, afraid if she touched him, he might shatter.

"It is not my intent to hurt you."

He took a bracing swallow of cognac before turning to face her. She had wrapped a blanket around her shoulders in an attempt at modesty. It failed. The blanket did nothing to shield her naked legs from view, and the memory of how they had felt clamped around his hips almost had him hurtling the glass into the fireplace.

"You know what they say, *ma cherie*. The road to hell is paved with good intentions."

She flinched, then reached for him. "Adrien, I—"

"You should go." He turned his back and sipped his drink. Inside, he was a cacophony of emotions, but damn if he would allow her to see how deep the wounds cut.

"You are being highly unreasonable. What of the countless women you have taken to bed? Did you believe all of them meant to become your bride?"

He spun around. "That was *sex*. Nothing more, and I am not quite the rogue you have always believed me to be. I imagine you think there have been hundreds of women in my bed, when in actuality I can count them on one hand." Her eyes widened. Good. She needed a dose of reality. "Having *you* in my bed was different. I thought you knew that. I thought I had made my feelings for you abundantly clear."

"Oh."

He gaped at her. "Oh? Oh! That is all you can manage to say?" He shook his head, unsure if he should be angry with her or feel sorry for her lack of understanding. "Do you love me, Eirene?"

"I told you I did." She kept her gaze averted, and her brow furrowed, as if still contemplating the information he had thrown at her.

"Then do us both a favor, hmm?"

She looked at him. "You wish me to leave."

Adrien set his drink down so he could take hold of both her shoulders. He tugged her closer, causing her grip on the blanket to slip. The heavy fabric slid down her right arm, nearly exposing her breast. God give him strength.

"I do not want you to leave. I want you to accept what is between us and agree to become my wife, because I cannot allow you to walk out of my life and I refuse to live as your kept man." Never mind he had enough money of his own, despite his exposure as a fraud. He needed to make a point. In spite of the remarkable pleasure of having her in his bed, he would not be used for sex. It was marriage or nothing, and God give him strength to accept the latter if that was what she chose.

"Adrien."

"Eirene."

She glowered at him, though the expression lacked fire. "You are very stubborn."

"Pot calling the kettle black, *ma cherie*."

"Adrien."

"Eirene." It occurred to him that he would counter her all day, if necessary.

She sighed. "I need time to think."

Hope pulsed through his veins. "I will allow you twenty-four hours. In that time, you will either return to my door or to the country. If you choose the latter, we shall never see one another again." The last words cost him dearly, and he did not miss the widening of her eyes or the movement of her neck as she swallowed.

"Very well. Twenty-four hours."

Chapter Nineteen

Dearest readers,

I leave the city for less than forty-eight hours and it seems all hell has broken loose. I apologize for abandoning you, and I shall do my best to inform you of all the delicious gossip that transpired during my absence.

It seems our roguish French Vicomte is not a Vicomte at all! You read correctly, dearest readers, the handsome Vicomte A. B. is but the son of a blacksmith! How fooled all of us were by his lovely manners and poetic countenance. I have no doubt, many a mamma is sighing with relief that their precious daughters were not bound in matrimony to the dashing, conniving wastrel!

And that is not all! As if lying about one's true identity were not enough, our false Vicomte was paid a late-night visit by none other than the reclusive and reckless Lady R-W! The "lady" was seen exiting our false Vicomte's house in what can only be described as a "huff." Let it be noted, her hair was shockingly unbound and she was sans pelisse and fichu!! One need not be a trained spy to deduce the meaning behind the absence of such wardrobe necessities.

I do believe doors will be closed to more than just our false Vicomte. I do believe the reclusive Lady R-W will never have the opportunity to fully enter Society, should she wish to.

I cannot speak for you, dearest readers, but I do not take kindly to being unwittingly involved in a game of lies and deceit! I cannot imagine Society will take kindly to it, either.

Heed my warning, "Vicomte" B and Lady R-W, Society does not forgive or forget easily…

On another, albeit less intriguing note, it seems the notoriously unpleasant, yet darkly handsome, Lord S. P. has departed our fine country for the distant shores of America. Again, I cannot speak for you, dearest readers, but I say, good riddance*!*

****

Eirene's hand trembled as she set the paper alongside her untouched breakfast plate. She stared at the cold toast and unappealing boiled egg. No doubt her tea had gone cold as well. Her appetite was nowhere to be found, and she wondered if it would ever return. Not that she cared one way or another if she ever ate again.

"Forgive me, Grandfather." She glanced across the room toward her grandfather's intimidating portrait. She'd opted for breakfast in her study, believing the comforting environs would improve her constitution. They had not. "I know it is most unlike me," she went on, addressing the portrait, "to have such a morose attitude, but how can I not?" She blinked rapidly as her eyes began to burn.

Adrien had given her a most unsatisfactory ultimatum. Twenty-four hours to agree to marriage or nothing. Why did the man have to be such a stubborn ass?!

The door opened, and Hamish entered, carrying a fresh pot of tea. He did nothing to hide his disappointed

231

expression as he glanced at her untouched breakfast. "Was something amiss with the food, my lady?"

"I would not know," she said, pushing the plate away. "I did not touch it."

Hamish frowned but said nothing. He had been with her long enough to interpret her moods, and the current mood begged for silence unless addressed directly.

Eirene sighed and sank back into the comfortable leather of her grandfather's oversized chair. "Tell me what to do, Hamish."

"In reference to…"

"Do not play coy, Hamish. It does not suit you." She straightened in the chair to prop her elbows upon the desk and her chin within her hands. "You know damn well what is plaguing my mind."

"The monsieur." Hamish motioned toward the nearest chair. "May I?"

Eirene granted permission with a nod, then watched as Hamish set the teapot on the desk and settled into the chair with a quiet sigh. She waited the length of a heartbeat. "Well?"

Hamish sighed again. Much louder this time. "Have you asked yourself what your grandfather would advise, my lady?"

"My grandfather would shoot the *monsieur* for defiling me." She did not miss the smirk Hamish tried, yet failed, to hide. "Does this amuse you, Hamish? Do you find my abject misery a source of great entertainment?"

His features sobered instantly. "Of course not, my lady, but if I may?"

"I insist that you do."

"It seems rather obvious your misery can be cured if only you would surrender to your feelings for the *monsieur*."

"I surrendered last night." Several times, in fact, but she did not believe Hamish required all the sordid details.

Hamish cleared his throat. "Quite. Only that is not what I meant."

"Yes, Hamish, I know." She allowed her gaze to stray beyond Hamish's shoulder, to her grandfather's portrait. Such a great man. He had taught her to fear nothing. No, that was not quite accurate. He had taught her to fear nothing but her feelings. As a result, she was terrified by the prospect of living with *or* without Adrien.

"You may go, Hamish."

"Very well, my lady."

Once alone, Eirene slid a fresh sheet of paper in front of her, dipped her pen, and began the most important list of her life.

****

Adrien watched as yet another shot went wide of the mark. He'd been playing billiards for what felt like hours, and he'd yet to sink one single damned ball. He blamed Eirene, the damned stubborn woman. She had stolen his ability to concentrate on the most menial of tasks. Of course, she had also stolen his heart and his sanity, but neither of those would win him money at the billiards table.

He leaned over the table, aimed and...*zut alors!*

The door opened just as Adrien thought to snap the stick over his thigh.

"Forgive the interruption, *monsieur*," Sayers

intoned the new moniker with all the deference due the former. At some point, Sayers had acquired the knowledge that Adrien was not a vicomte. Nothing had been said beyond the simple change of address. "You have a visitor."

Adrien's heart actually stopped. Was it possible? Had Eirene ret—

Westhaven strolled into the room before Sayers could announce him.

His heart began beating once more as disappointment soured his mood. "Westhaven, I'm shocked you would risk your reputation in such a fashion."

Westhaven snorted and shooed Sayers from the room. "As if I have a stellar reputation to protect?" He thrust a bottle toward Adrien. "Fresh off the boat," he said with a wink. "Shall we test its worth?"

Adrien willingly abandoned his game to fetch two glasses.

Westhaven poured, swirled, sniffed, and finally took a swallow of the rich amber-colored cognac. "Worth the risk every time," he said with a smack of his lips.

"*Oui*, very fine," Adrien agreed after a sip he barely tasted.

Westhaven's gaze became invasive. "My God, man, you look as volatile as Venton at the moment. What has happened?"

"Have you not read the papers, Henry?"

Westhaven gestured with his glass. "Of course, of course, but who cares about all that vicomte nonsense? I'm sure you had your reasons for embarking upon such an elaborate masquerade." He paused, as if expecting

Adrien to enumerate said reasons. After a few moments of silence, he shrugged and continued, "Your dark mood has nothing to do with the clubs closing their doors to you."

"Perhaps it is due to my tailor closing his doors as well?"

"Oh, yes, of course." Westhaven rolled his eyes, took another drink, and sat on the edge of the billiard table. "I am your friend, Adrien, not an imbecile. Talk to me."

Adrian looked at Westhaven. The sincerity in the man's brown eyes could not be ignored. "I am in love with Lady Rowe-Weston."

"I know."

"You—"

Westhaven laughed. "God, Adrien, you are not *that* good of an actor. She is a spectacular woman. Of course, you are in love with her."

There was too much in Westhaven's *logic* to consider right now, so Adrien simply ignored all of it. "I proposed marriage. Twice, or maybe three times—"

"And she refused."

"If you know everything, why am I talking?"

Westhaven laughed in the face of his ire. "At ease, my friend. You proposed, she refused. Go on."

"I gave her an ultimatum. Twenty-four hours to choose to be my wife or we never see one another again."

Westhaven whistled. "And was this ultimatum meant to make her life a living hell or merely your own?"

"Bugger off, Westhaven."

"No, thank you." Westhaven saluted Adrien with

his glass and flashed an annoyingly charismatic smile. "How many hours has it been?"

"I don't know." Adrien took a seat as well on the edge of the table and stared into his drink. "The woman is more stubborn than a pack of mules. She will live in solitary misery before ever surrendering to the confines of marriage." He glanced over at Westhaven. "If I could, I would dig up her grandfather's remains and challenge the man to a duel for ruining the life of such an amazing woman."

"Has it not occurred to you, she would not be the woman you love if not for the influence of her grandfather, not that I have any idea what you are referring to, of course, but people become who they are based on the—"

"Do shut up, Westhaven."

Henry clamped his lips around his glass, somehow managing to laugh and drink at the same time.

"Why are you here, tormenting me? Isn't Miss Parish in need of stalking?"

"That is cruel, but I will forgive you because of your current state of mind."

Sayers appeared without warning. "Monsieur, a letter has arrived for you." He held out a folded piece of paper. No envelope, no seal. He left before Adrien could ask questions.

"Rather informal," Westhaven remarked without cause.

Adrien balanced his drink on the edge of the table and opened the paper. The sight of Eirene's handwriting accelerated his heart beat and heated the blood in his veins. The words blurred. *Jesu*, was this a refusal? In writing?

"Go away, Westhaven."

"No, I believe I will remain."

Adrien barely heard Henry's refusal as he blinked to try and bring the words into focus. Columns. The paper had been divided into two columns. An odd way to format a rejection letter. The two large words at the top came into focus—Cons and Pros

He frowned at the order of the words. Didn't one normally list the advantages before the disadvantages? And Cons and Pros of what?

"Are you going to read it or scowl at it until I read it for you?"

Adrien shot a glare toward Henry, who now hovered at his elbow. "I told you to leave."

"And I decided to stay." Henry poked the back of the paper with his index finger. "Go on, read it before I expire of curiosity."

And so Adrien began to read. Half way through, he wished Henry was not privy to Eirene's list, but in for a penny, in for a pound.

The Cons and Pros of accepting Adrien's marriage proposal

Cons: He is a commoner/Grandfather would not approve

He is now a social outcast/We would be invited nowhere

He makes me lose my reason/And a woman without reason is weak

I love him/Love destroys

Pros: He is a commoner/And commoners value love and family above money and rank

He is a social outcast/Which means we could enjoy a peaceful life in the country

He makes me lose reason/And it is a most exhilarating feeling

I love him/And my world would be empty without his smiling eyes, boyish smile, accented voice, and delectable collarbone

In conclusion: Will you marry me, Monsieur Adrien Coultier?

Adrien shoved the list into Henry's chest as he brushed past him on his way to the door.

Henry dogged his heels. "You mean to send a reply, yes?"

"No." He never broke stride as he called for Sayers to fetch his hat and gloves. The man appeared with suspicious speed, but he was too preoccupied to care. He paused at the door to look back at Henry. "Tell Cyril I've gone to fetch my bride."

****

Eirene stood at the window of her breakfast room, staring out at the street. She'd been trembling uncontrollably since handing the list off to Hamish with instructions to have it delivered to Adrien. Had she completely lost her mind? What if the infuriating man read the list, laughed, and tossed it into the fire?

She pressed her fist to her chest. Gracious, could a human heart beat any faster?

"My lady?"

She turned from the window with enough speed to tangle her skirts with the curtains. She did not care. "Hamish? Yes? What is—"

Adrien stepped around Hamish. Her heart stopped and started again with a painful palpitation.

He strolled toward her, eyes smiling, boyish grin firmly in place. *"Oui, ma cherie. Oui."*

Upon reaching her, he took her in his arms and embraced her with enough force to steal her breath. He buried his face in her hair and found her ear with his lips. "I love you."

Eirene smiled. Though Adrien wore all the proper layers of clothing, she could feel the unmistakable ridge of his collarbone. Turning her face, she nuzzled the area with her nose. He was hers to do with as she desired. Whenever and wherever. And now seemed like a lovely time to exercise said claim.

Stepping back, she reached for the buttons of his collar while meeting his gaze. "I want to make love to you."

He arched a brow. "Here? Now?" His gaze strayed toward the very public window.

"Oui." Having finished with the buttons, Eirene began to push his jacket from his shoulders. Of course, the fit was exceptional, making it a tad difficult to remove. "Help me, Adrien, for heaven's sake."

He did, and with amusing speed. Standing before her in naught but his well-tailored, black trousers and riding boots, he held his arms out and flashed a gloriously, roguish smile. "I am at your service, my lady. Now and forever."

A word about the author…

When not writing stories of happily ever after, Lora spends her time reading, listening to music, drinking way too much coffee and rocking out behind her drums.